Allan Massie was born in Singapore and educated at
Glenalmond and Trinity College, Cambridge. The author of
One Night in Winter, he has been acclaimed as one of
Scotland's finest novelists.

Trinity SRobb.
Elverham,
July 1988

Also by Allan Massie

Novels

ONE NIGHT IN WINTER
THE LAST PEACOCK
THE DEATH OF MEN

Non-Fiction

MURIEL SPARK
ILL MET BY GASLIGHT
THE CAESARS
EDINBURGH AND THE BORDERS: AN ANTHOLOGY (Ed)

ALLAN MASSIE

Change and Decay in All Around I See

Futura

For Alison, who contradicts the title

A Futura Book

Copyright © Allan Massie 1978

First published in Great Britain in 1978
by The Bodley Head Ltd

This edition published in 1986
by Futura Publications, a Division of
Macdonald & Co (Publishers) Ltd
London & Sydney

ISBN 0 7088 2753 5

Printed and bound in Great Britain by
Collins, Glasgow

Futura Publications
a Division of
Macdonald & Co (Publishers) Ltd
Greater London House
Hampstead Road
London NW1 7QX

A BPCC plc Company

I

'My first disobedience,' sighed Atwater—but it was no good —'was the fruit . . .'

He passed his hand, palm outward, across his dripping brow.

'Too long ago, that's for sure,' he said.

With his left hand he re-adjusted the towel. This room was decidedly too hot, hellishly so. He could never remember which room was which. In fact, even now, after weeks, he was uncertain of the lay-out of the Baths.

He looked across the room. A large purple man was extended belly upward on the bench. Somewhere in the distance or perhaps the Past a man was singing,

'As I stroll along the Bois de Boulogne, with an independent air,
You can hear the girls declare, "He must be a millionaire";
You can hear them sigh and wish to die,
You can see them wink the other eye
At the man who broke the Bank at Monte Carlo.'

Straw boater, pink carnation, spats . . . he must be in the Past, it was too hot for him here . . .

'My first disobedience . . .' Atwater tried again . . . 'did apples enter it?'

Or was that merely something he had read? Were there such things as universal, all-purpose myths? A matter to ponder on . . .

Atwater was in the hottest room of the Baths. Drunk when he entered, he had forgotten his sandals. His entering feet had been insensitive to the heat of the tiles. They would be scalded as he left. And if he didn't depart, he might pass out.

'Life,' as he had informed an acolyte in Finch's earlier in the evening, 'is a succession of passing-out parades.'

The acolyte had been impressed.

'But,' Atwater had continued, frowning over his spectacles, 'we do not know the drill. The angelic sergeant has welshed on us.'

The purple man opposite rose, whoofling.

'The world is too much with us,' he said. 'Or so I've heard tell.'

Atwater nodded assent. He was left alone. An almost palpable silence, like an Edwardian fog, hung over the Baths. Atwater was aware of the brooding presence of night, like a spirit over a vast abyss. At this hour he felt the presence of the sleeping millions, far more urgent than during their diurnal labours. The night was ever pregnant of possibility. Hail, heavenly night . . . up to a point.

For the last few weeks Atwater had been living in the Savoy Turkish Baths in Jermyn Street. If anyone asked why, he said, 'It's convenient and they ask no questions.'

This made many people think he was queer, which wasn't true. Atwater's sexual urge was weak, had been for years. Occasionally, perhaps twice a month, he masturbated. Then he sometimes entertained images of flagellation; but he never came near responding to one of those advertisements which offer firm discipline or severe treatment.

The fact was he had gone to the Baths the night he came out of prison and found they suited him. Prison had been congenial enough too. He had arrived there because a number of optimistically post-dated cheques had eventually found their way to his bank and been speedily and repeatedly returned with the banal suggestion that they be referred to Drawer. There followed what Atwater termed 'a bit of unpleasantness', in the course of which with quite uncharacteristic violence he struck one of his creditors, a Greek-Cypriot restaurant proprietor. He got three months.

He shared a cell with an alcoholic Irish labourer (taking, he assumed, a cure the hard way) and a Jamaican con-man. He found both quite as agreeable as most of the people he

6

knew; particularly the Irishman, who was not only able to advise him on the finer points of prison etiquette but never interrupted Atwater's frequently lengthy monologues. Nor was the food any worse than much that he'd been accustomed to—certainly than the Cypriot's. Most of all though he liked having no decisions to make.

When he was released and they gave him his clothes back he took a train to London. That wasn't really a decision either. He'd hardly left London in years. Other people took holidays in St Tropez or Torremolinos; Atwater merely dived deeper into Earl's Court.

Yet he had a purpose.

The week before he left prison he had received a letter from a firm of solicitors in Woburn Place. It wasn't the sort of solicitor's letter to which he was accustomed. Rather it informed him that they, Messrs Wilkins, Hodgson, Prendergast and Wilkins, were the trustees for the Estate of his grandmother who, they were sorry to have to report, had died a couple of weeks back in the St Asaph's Home for Decayed Gentlewomen, Tunbridge Wells. Since the old lady's faculties had so decayed as to preclude any recognition of others for at least seven years, Atwater couldn't pretend to feel any great sorrow, though he had been fond of her up to the age of eight. More important, the letter stated that he was sole legatee. The sum wasn't large—Mrs Atwater had been a clergyman's widow—but it might amount to about £4000. It seemed quite considerable to Atwater who couldn't remember when he had last had a credit balance of a hundred and fifty.

So it was with an air of triumph that he took the tube to Bloomsbury. 'Thou has put down the mighty from their seat and hast exalted the humble and meek', as they used to chant with gusto at school chapel. (Not Atwater though; he mumbled his way through the Psalms and was dumb in the responses.)

The solicitors' office came as something of a shock to him. He had expected them to be fuggy and inhabited by pince-nezed clerks blowing the dust off deeds. Instead he found himself before a glass-and-concrete tower that pierced the

7

smoky blue of the autumn sky. He was directed to the seventh floor and a blonde girl in a camel-coloured dress with white collar and cuffs told him that young Mr Wilkins would see him in ten minutes and would he mind waiting. Atwater, courteous and obedient, not-at-alled and sat down and rolled himself a cigarette. He had got quite good at doing this without a machine in prison and didn't see why he should abandon the habit.

The blonde girl asked him if he would like a cup of coffee.

'I'm just going to have one myself,' she said. 'There's really nothing else to do here.'

'We'd some difficulty tracing you,' she said.

The letter had been forwarded from several addresses.

'I came here as soon as I could,' Atwater replied.

'You're very good at rolling cigarettes,' she said. 'I don't have the patience.'

'It's just a knack,' said Atwater, consciously modest.

'I hope it's not pot?'

'Pot?'

'Not that it matters. I don't mind and Jeremy's far too innocent and his uncle's out and Mr Prendergast's senile.'

'Jeremy?'

'Young Mr Wilkins. That's what we have to call him in the office. Tell you what. I can't open the window 'cause they don't, but I'll put on this. That'll clear the air.'

She depressed a switch and a mighty rushing sound boomed around the room.

'Gives you a headache, doesn't it?' she shouted.

'Yes.'

A door at the far end of the room opened and a ridiculously pink young man came in. His suit was severely striped; someone with his interests at heart should have advised him against wearing a shirt the colour of grilled salmon. He shouted,

'Mr Atwater?'

Atwater stood up.

'Anthony Rupert Atwater?'

8

Atwater inclined his head and the youth beckoned. Atwater followed him into an office not much larger than the cell he had that morning left.

'I wasn't a partner when we moved in,' young Mr Wilkins said. 'Now can you identify yourself?'

'Identify myself?'

'Yes. You know, driving licence, passport, credit cards, anything like that'll do. Got to have identification. Make sure we have the right Atwater. Beware of impostors, you know.'

Atwater was momentarily flummoxed. He had none of these things. Why should he? He'd never wanted to drive or leave the country; and, deeply attractive though he found the idea of credit cards, his sole request for one had caused his bank manager's upper lip to curl so high it had all but got involved with his eyeball.

'My National Insurance number is YM461632A,' he said.

'That's impressive.' Young Mr Wilkins seemed indeed quite overcome by this display of knowledge. 'But . . . red tape, you know. Takes time to check. They have to send all the way to Newcastle. Can you believe that?'

They sat in silence for a moment. Then Atwater, feeling this identification business had gone far enough, said,

'I was sorry I couldn't get to the funeral.'

'Funeral?'

'There was a funeral, I take it.'

'Burnt,' said Mr Wilkins. 'Perfectly proper. Woking.'

'I've never liked the idea of cremation myself. Strange, isn't it? And into ashes all my lust. Not that that's very applicable to my grandma. Not as far as I know. Certainly not in recent years. Suttee, of course, was a perfectly respectable Hindu practice and must have avoided a lot of bother. I never have understood why we suppressed it. Liberal love of meddling, I expect. Of course that used to take place immediately after the husband's death, which would have knocked a bit off my grandma's life. He died in 1919. Spanish 'flu.'

9

Mr Wilkins was biting his fingernails with some energy.

'Tricky, this identification biznai. Can't be too wary of impostors.'

'What I was wondering though,' Atwater said, 'is whether it mightn't be possible for you to give me an advance. I'm a bit short at the moment. I know about probate and all that, but I thought perhaps, a few hundred pounds.'

'Nothing easier, squire. Only there's this identification diffy.'

Atwater began to feel that all was slipping away. It was like one of those nightmares he'd read about—he never had nightmares himself—in which the dreamer is forever reaching out to grasp an object which forever eludes him.

'I wouldn't be here if I wasn't Atwater. Anthony Rupert Atwater.'

There was a certain defiance in his tone because he'd never much cared for his names and indeed they were rarely used.

Mr Wilkins examined his right hand, presumably found it satisfactory and commenced gnawing operations on the left.

'What about lunch?' he said after a few bites.

'I'd be delighted to give you lunch, but unless you advance me some of my money, I'm afraid it's out of the question. Indeed, I don't know where I shall sleep tonight.'

'No, no, when you lunch with your solicitor, your solicitor pays. Matter of principle. Tradition too. Course, I don't say you won't find it on your bill, but we've got to observe formalities. Tell you what, we'll take Clare.'

He shouted into a speaking-tube.

'Clarici, lunchers.'

Atwater was mildly perturbed, but not despairing. Long years of borrowing had forced him to acknowledge that financial transactions were frequently protracted. And, moreover, he was hungry. He had breakfasted at six-thirty. A drink wouldn't be unwelcome either. Several drinks, in fact. He was after all a good many behind.

They went out to a pub which had not escaped redevelopment. Young Mr Wilkins greeted the barmaid as an old friend but she didn't respond. The pub was stuffy with a smell of polish and shepherd's pie. Atwater looked disapprovingly over the top of his horn-rimmed spectacles at the regiment of stripe-suited backs that lined the bar. Nobody took any notice of his disapproval. This look had led his comrades in the nick to call him 'Prof.'.

The first swallow of his large pink gin restored his equilibrium. It was clear to him that he must settle this matter of an advance here in the pub. Battles should be fought on ground of your own choosing. He rolled another cigarette. The girl, Clare, said,

'Could I have one of those, please?'

'But of course.'

'You look worried,' she said.

'The times are worrying,' said Atwater. 'We live in a changing world.'

'Better than a changing-room,' said young Mr Wilkins returning to their table and guffawing. 'Shall we go through and get some scoff?'

They had a bottle of Beaujolais from one of the better Algerian factories with their shepherd's pie.

'Some brandy?'

'You've got an appointment with your uncle at four o'clock, Jeremy,' Clare said.

'Miserable old man. Can still have some brandy. Kip for an hour or two, can't I? Lunching a client. Must have some brandy.'

He beckoned wildly.

'Three double brandies.'

'With soda,' said Atwater. 'For me at least.'

'Atwater,' said young Mr Wilkins. 'You're all right.'

'About this advance,' said Atwater. 'I have no money at the moment, you see. None. Therefore, if you could arrange . . .'

'It's just this identification. It worries me, Atwater, it worries me.'

'Take my word for it.'

'Of course he's Atwater. Jeremy, you've got to learn to trust people.'

'All right then, we'll chance it. It's false pretences if you're not Atwater. You'll go to prison, you know.'

'Prison has no terrors for me. Make the cheque open.'

'Will two hundred do?'

'Adequately, for the moment.'

'I daren't make it more. Not till we've got the identification biznai settled.'

It was a long time since Atwater had had as much as two hundred pounds and after he had cashed his cheque he couldn't think what to do. He sat down on a bench and counted the money again. It was three o'clock and late September and golden. Atwater riffled through the notes and put them in his inside pocket and buttoned it. He sat on the bench. Nothing to happen till five-thirty. The blessed interstices of England. He wondered if there was anyone he could go and see. That was all a long time in the past and in a sense he was beginning a new life. He couldn't think of anything he wasn't free from. Two hundred pounds at ten pounds a day would last three weeks, counting Sundays cheap. There was a betting-shop across the road. Waiting till the lights changed he was just in time to invest on the three-thirty. Ten pounds to win at ten to one. Three hundred pounds at ten pounds a day would last a month, no need to stint himself on Sundays.

He didn't stay there having at that moment no belief in a run of luck.

By five-twenty-seven Atwater was in the Fulham Road, waiting for the iron gates of Finch's to be unlocked. Meanwhile he glanced with disapproval at the window of an antique shop. At one time in his life he had collected English china; in a small way. Later he had worked for a few months in a shop just like this. That had been more satisfactory. Eventually however his use of the float to finance his lunch-time and early evening sessions had become careless.

By six o'clock he was outside two pints of draught Guinness and talking to an Australian who had once been a cartoonist on a Darwin paper. The conversation was pleasantly contrapuntal. The Australian, whose name was Richie, talked about alimony; Atwater about prison.

'It's amazing how quickly you assimilate and identify.'

'So she thinks she can screw me for another five hundred because she's gone to live in bleeding Chiswick.'

'Some of the screws are real villains.'

'Stuff it, Sheila, I say, nobody told you you 'ad to leave Notting Hill.'

'I met a very nice blind burglar who told me the most appalling stories.'

'You're a real cow if you think I'm going to support you in a higher standard of living now than when we were married. That's what I told the bitch.'

'You wouldn't believe the perversions you find in the prison service. *Droit de seigneur* isn't . . .'

'Look, I said, you're forgetting, I've got to pay alimony to Karen too now.'

'You have unbridled sexual appetites,' said Atwater. 'Why don't you go to prison for a bit? It will give you a new perspective. The world would be a better place if everyone—two pints please, Jerry—went to prison from time to time—yes, Guinness it is—particularly politicians. It's the only place you find original thought.'

'And now I'm shacked up with Sarah. Not that I told her that, but it's another difficulty, see.'

'My God, it's that swine Atwater,' said a stout, balding man in a maroon boiler-suit and wire-framed glasses that were slipping down his nose.'

'Horridge,' Atwater said.

'You can buy me a pint.'

'But of course.'

Atwater, *beau sabreur* of the saloon bar, delved in his pockets. He had known Horridge for years, although

Horridge was considerably younger. This wasn't immediately apparent because he wasn't wearing well. His complexion was curiously mottled. Atwater had first met him one New Year's morning in a drinking-club in Gravesend. They had been playing spoof . . . later Atwater had fallen backwards off a bar-stool. He had been awakened to find himself on a strange sofa (though he had in fact woken on so many unknown sofas that the experience could never be entirely strange). A large, dark, German girl with a fine moustache was shaking him and demanding three pounds so that she could return to London.

'It doesn't cost three pounds,' he had said and attempted to return to sleep. With Teutonic persistence she had prevented this and Atwater had given her a reluctant pound.

''E's a bloody swine that Horridge,' she had said.

Later in the day Atwater and Horridge had breakfasted off brandy, Bass and kipper pâté. Atwater described his morning encounter.

'*Quelle* bitch,' said Horridge, but didn't offer to repay the pound.

That had been the beginning of their acquaintance which had blossomed, a few months subsequently, when they collaborated in an unprincipled attempt to foist a peculiarly sickly ersatz German champagne on the British public. Meeting with obduracy, the bulldog spirit, they had drunk most of their samples themselves and faded from the scene. For the next few months, in the Shepherd Market area, Atwater turned corners cautiously, fearful of encountering Herr Durkelheim, the brand's promoter.

'Where have you been, Atwater?' Horridge said. 'The pubs have missed you.'

'I've been in prison.'

'Join the club.'

'You been back?'

'Not recently.'

Horridge was an old lag; arson his favourite crime; there was some acceptable psychological explanation, so he was more accustomed to nut-houses than ordinary nicks. Nevertheless his ready ability to become either drunk and disorderly or drunk and incapable had ensured that he had a fairly wide experience of the cells, both in the United Kingdom and on the Continent. Many people found Horridge a nuisance. He had lately taken to proclaiming revolutionary politics.

'It was extraordinarily interesting,' Atwater said, turning his back against the bar, the better to hold his audience in thrall. 'I've just been telling Richie here that in my opinion a short course of prison life would do everyone a power of good.'

'Widens the horizons,' nodded Horridge.

'Christ, you oughta see the nick in Wagga Wagga.'

'I don't think the where matters,' Atwater said.

Atwater, at home, let the orchestra of the bar play around him. Horridge and the Australian were launched on discussion as Horridge attempted to ascertain the revolutionary potentialities of the Australian aborigines. Atwater didn't listen. A very ugly man, reminiscent of Field-Marshal von Hindenberg, passed by, scowling.

'That man's not nearly as nice as he looks,' Atwater said.

'It's sex the abos are good at, not politics,' said Richie.

Horridge's glasses were slipping farther down his nose, sure sign of incipient intoxication.

'This pub's going downhill,' he muttered, suddenly gloomy.

'Downhill all the way,' echoed Atwater happily. 'The image of existence.'

A small goatee-bearded man turned from his *Evening News* and said to Atwater,

'D'you know about the man who went to his doctor and said he couldn't hear?'

'No,' said Atwater. 'I'm glad to say I don't.'

The small man frowned, possibly in reproach.

'The doctor examined him, see. You drink too much, he said to the man.'

'Don't we all?'

'Stop drinking and you'll be all right. So the man goes away and goes on the wagon and in a month he's completely cured.'

'This is intolerable,' said Atwater.

'Six weeks later the man comes back. Can't hear a thing, he says.'

'Oh God!'

'That's funny, says the doc, I thought you'd be all right when you stopped drinking. Oh yes, says the man, but I found I liked what I was hearing so much less than what I was drinking that I went back to drinking again. Good, isn't it?'

'Hilarious,' said Atwater.

'I'm the man,' said goatee-beard. 'Curse me as much as you like, I can't hear a thing. Large brandy and ginger-ale.'

Horridge put his face very close to goatee-beard.

'Do you want to be smashed?' he said.

'Can't hear a thing,' giggled goatee-beard.

'Good heavens, there's my solicitor,' said Atwater.

Horridge looked at him with respect.

'Which? Who? Where?'

'That very pink young man.'

'He's very young.'

'And pink.'

'I like the bird.'

Atwater waved a compelling arm and young Mr Wilkins and Clare pushed their way through the ever-thickening throng. He greeted Atwater like a brother of whom he was more than usually fond.

'Atwater, it's good to see you, Atwater, you're a good friend, Atwater. Clarici, you remember old Atwater, Rupert.'

All doubts of identity seemed to have been stilled.

'Is this man an officer of the court?' inquired Horridge.

'I've no idea.'

The evening continued. Later they all crossed the road to eat a pizza and drink dubious Valpolicella. Young Mr

Wilkins was with difficulty inserted into a taxi and restrained from emerging by the other door. Clare assured them she could manage and directed the driver to Islington. Atwater said to Horridge,

'How drunk the young get.'

He remembered that and then he woke up in the Turkish Baths.

Atwater's life soon fell into a routine. He woke around eight and rang for tea. Then he lay there, smoking and sipping, watching men with hangovers straighten out and prepare to go to their offices. Some of them looked sheepish, others smug. When the first batch was cleared he took a little snooze, then got up and padded to shave. He came back and chatted in philosophical style to Mac, the little snowy-haired Glaswegian cleaner who officiated in the ground-floor dormitory during the day. Mac was a more or less retired alcoholic who spent a good part of the morning studying form in *The Sporting Life*. This conversation made Atwater feel he had a share in the decisions of the day; it also passed the time till eleven-twenty when he would set off to have a pint in the Red Lion in Duke of York Street while it was still quiet and you could enjoy the glass. He would then proceed to Piccadilly Circus and take the underground to South Kensington. Depending on the weather he would walk or take a bus to the Queen's Elm. The length of his stay there was decided by the company he found but generally he had reached Finch's by one o'clock where he remained, with occasional excursions to the betting-shop, until three-fifteen. The afternoon was passed either in the betting-shop or in the ABC cinema if he felt a little sleepy. At five-twenty-eight he was on duty again outside the iron gates. And so to the garrulous evening, concluding with the taxi back to Jermyn Street, the half-hour in the hot-room, the cold plunge and perhaps the massage, the cup of heavily laced tea and nature's last balm, slumber.

He was quite happy living like this and didn't consider the future.

Curiously he met with consistent success in the betting-shop. He developed—or had wished on him by a higher power—a knack of picking the winners of two-mile novice hurdles. Atwater, humble in certain areas, recognised this as a mystery and was careful to sprinkle a few drops of liquor on the floor of Finch's before heading for the bookie; fortunately it was a pub where such action appeared neither bizarre nor reprehensible. Most of the staff were Irish and realised that if this was the way a man picked winners, it was the way a man picked winners. The argument carried for them all the cogent logic that the Iron Laws of Economics did for Mr Gradgrind, etc. Also Atwater was not the man to conceal his decisions.

He began to be respected in the betting-shop. People hovered near him, wheezing eagerly, as he made out his slip. A large and loquacious Jamaican called Aloysius generously pressed appalling recommendations of arthritic chasers on him only demanding in return a share in Atwater's arcane knowledge. Aloysius indeed believed quite openly that Atwater had a link-up with the Powers of Darkness and offered to assist here too.

'Ah know where to buy black cockerels real dirt cheap, man,' he said. 'Dem's genuine free-range cockerels too, take my assurance, none of dem battery trash. Ain't no good sacrificing battery trash.'

'You mistake my methods,' Atwater replied.

Others were similarly affected. One day in early November (a difficult meeting at Haydock), Atwater was surprised to feel a hand touch the hem of the mid-calf-length, navy-blue overcoat he was wearing. Looking down, he saw a very small Irishman kneeling. He was pretending to tie the bit of string that served him as a shoelace but Atwater knew better.

'I distinctly felt the virtue go out of me,' he told Horridge severely.

'Jesus Christ,' said Horridge, impressed.

'Quite.'

The result of all this success was that Atwater found none of the expected necessity to call on young Mr Wilkins. He was happy to think on no basis at all that his money was fructifying. However, Mr Wilkins and Clare were frequently to be met with in the pubs. Indeed they seemed to have attached themselves to Atwater. Clare liked to consult him.

'She views me as an oracle,' Atwater told Horridge.

'I had a girl like that once,' he replied. 'She was quite a girl. Do you know what gave her her biggest kicks?'

Atwater shuddered.

'She liked me to lie across her, both of us starkers natch, and put grapes in my mouth. Drop them in, one by one.'

'Black or green?'

'Didn't worry her. I tell you it was fucking erotic.'

Richie leant across the counter, sideways.

'Wasn't an abo, was she?'

'No, her father was a chemist in Tooting. Sadly respectable family, petit bourgeois slugs as a matter of fact.'

'Been interesting if she'd been an abo. Mind you, I'd expect an abo to prefer prickly pears.'

Clare was curious about Atwater's past too.

'Murky,' he assured her.

'Why haven't you ever married? I can tell you're not queer.'

Atwater was curious as to how she knew. He asked her.

'You're so funny, Atwater,' she said. 'Queers are never funny like that.'

This mystified Atwater who knew some tolerably amusing homosexuals.

'That's what's wrong with Jeremy, you know.'

They were, rather unusually, having dinner together, alone in an Indian restaurant. Atwater was a little uncertain. He had a suspicion he had been outmanoeuvred. Clare was a charming girl, but giving girls dinner wasn't Atwater's style; not even in Indian restaurants that looked like the mess of an unfashionable regiment that had made a poor showing in the Afghan Wars. They were alone in the restaurant except for two waiters. As usual, one was skinny, the other obese. The skinny child was hard at work, picking his nose. It had taken skill on Atwater's part to be served by the fat one.

'What's wrong with Jeremy?' he repeated.

'Yes, well you see, Atwater, it's like this, he wonders if he wouldn't be happier being queer again. He used to be queer at Eton of course and had such fun with his fag I suppose he thinks he was much happier then. So he wonders if he should go back to boys. I must say it would be bliss not going to bed with him.'

'Really?'

'It's not sex I mind, that's fun and he's not bad you know in a schoolboyish sort of way. It's afterwards. He's sentimental about sleeping together, meaning sleeping. Really you know I think that part's somehow more important to him than fucking, something about waking together he says— all right, I say waking if you've ever managed to get to sleep— but it's terrible, you can't imagine, Atwater. I used to have a sweet bulldog you know and he always slept in my bed, the lamb, but having Jeremy's more like a St Bernard, only he snores like a rhinoceros and kicks like one—assuming they do, that is. So you see it would be easier if he went back to being queer. Trouble is, he's not very attractive to queers. I mean, you couldn't call Jeremy pretty, could you?'

'No.'

'And he's not rich either. And it seems to me you must have a pretty thin time as a queer if you're not pretty and you're not rich. So what would you advise?'

Atwater crumbled a thoughtful poppadum.

'I think he should go back to Eton,' he said.

'You're so funny, Atwater.'

This conversation left Atwater, to his surprise, feeling

flattered and a little perplexed. People had not been accustomed to tell him secrets. He wondered if he had in some way been offered an invitation. To be an uncle perhaps; surely not a sugar-daddy. He began also to watch how young Mr Wilkins spoke to barmen. It was difficult to come to any conclusion. Atwater had been told too many lies in too many pubs to place any credence in that old nonsense of *in vino veritas*.

'Depend upon it,' he was wont to say, 'the man who coined that phrase was drunk.'

'But,' said a young man standing at his unexpected elbow one evening, 'you're drunk yourself now.'

'Quite,' said Atwater, 'who are you anyway?'

'We've met before,' said the young man. 'You could call me an effectual angel. Listen to this.'

'Certainly not. You say we've met before?'

'Often. Let me tell you a story.'

'Where have we met?'

'Here, there, everywhere. The heroine of my story, a young girl who sold cream tarts.'

'Cream tarts?'

'There. I knew you'd be interested.'

'Nothing of the kind.'

'Atwater.'

'You know my name?'

'How else could I call you Atwater? Your life is without form.'

The young man had a cast in his left eye, his features were Jewish and he was drinking Bass.

'I'm writing a novel,' said the young man.

'Oh God,' said Atwater, 'oh Montreal.'

'You're a character. It will give form to your life. Tell me about it and I'll introduce you to the girl who sold cream tarts. As a matter of fact I'll let you into a secret, sells not sold, she's still at it. Shall I go on?'

The young man's appearance was becoming more grotesque minute by minute. His left hand was missing a finger and his eye-teeth were unnaturally prominent.

'She's a dear girl,' he said, 'more than usually expensive. Not just for the price of a cream tart you'll buy her. Actually your turning-up is a godsend. I was wondering how she was to be rescued from her predicament. She's in trouble.'

Atwater looked at the barman who didn't seem to be there —it must be a club of some sort he'd got himself into—to order a desperate drink. There was a candle on the bar standing in a mock-rococo stick. He raised it head-high as they used to do in the days of studio movies. The young man was looking at him intently with an amber eye. He raised a tube like a tooth-brush made into a pencil.

'You're the only Public School man in the pub, Atwater.'

Atwater's hand went to his neck where he felt constricted. He asked the barman who wasn't there for a brandy and soda.

'The cream tarts are depressed'—the young man's accent had become thickly foreign—'there's this young undertaker's undertaken to get them in trouble. Atwater, for the honour of the school.'

'*Nemo me impune arcessit*,' said Atwater sipping his brandy (and how had it got into his hand?).

But there was something wrong.

'I knew there was something wrong,' he said to Mac in the morning. 'That wasn't our motto even if I'd got it right.'

'I bleeding well think no,' said Mac. 'Aye it's a strange world, Mr Atwater.'

'There are mornings I agree and other times I find the strangeness has worn off in the course of my thirty-eight years. The young man was impertinent though. I'll give him a set-down should we meet again. Curious, too, that he knew who I was.'

'Ye're a weel-kent loon.' Mac commenced desultory operations with a mop and bucket. 'There's mair kens Tam Fool; ah weel, we're a' Jock Tamson's bairns as the crack gangs.'

'That's easily seen,' said a stout red-moustachioed figure emerging like a walrus from the steam room. 'You're

22

Atwater, the gambler. I'm Colonel Beazley, the celebrated swine.'

Atwater sat down on his bunk and put his head in his hands.

'They should reserve the day till the afternoon,' he said.

'If you give me five minutes, we'll go and have a jar,' said Colonel Beazley. 'I've had my eye on you, Atwater, and I want a chat.'

Atwater found his instincts advising him to be off. Mere anarchy, they remarked shaking their heads like a skein of maiden aunts, is loosed upon the world.

'We'll go to the Hyde Park Hotel,' said the soi-disant swine. 'They make tolerable champagne cocktails there and even the Ritz is full of counter-jumpers these days. It's about marriage I want your opinion. My wife or my daughter?'

Atwater was flummoxed, an unusual condition. He followed Colonel Beazley reluctantly into Jermyn Street. He felt like one in the grip of some ineluctable fate. He had no desire to discuss marriage. Colonel Beazley opened the door of a grey Bentley which had just drawn up at the kerb.

'In you get,' he snapped.

Atwater obeyed. The driver, a thin young man looking depressingly like one of Nature's blunders, an evolutionary cul-de-sac, turned round, making the effect worse. His mouth dropped.

'Take us,' said Colonel Beazley, 'to the Hyde Park Hotel. And look sharp about it.'

'But . . .' said the young man.

Colonel Beazley leaned across Atwater and stabbed his forefinger in the young man's neck.

'You're already pointing in that direction,' he said.

'My mother . . . Fortnums,' the youth whimpered.

'Bah,' said Colonel Beazley.

The young man let in the clutch. Colonel Beazley began to gnaw the handle of his umbrella. Atwater considered the advisability of commending his soul to God, and decided the time was not yet ripe. They arrived at the hotel.

'My compliments to your mama, young feller,' said the

Colonel. 'Beazley's the name.' He sounded positively florid. They descended to the bar.

Atwater considered the Colonel as his host engaged himself in detailed instructions to the barman. It appeared that no one else in London could make champagne cocktails. It was a lost art, like moving pillars of rock by solar rays. Atwater wouldn't have been surprised if Colonel Beazley had been well up in that too. He was tempted to break the habit of a lifetime and entertain curiosity. He fought against it. Down, wanton, down.

Beazley said, 'Afraid I startled you. Shock tactics you know. I remember Monty telling me, have another drink when you feel the need, there's a whole jug made.'

'The Field-Marshal said that?'

'Time and again. No, Atwater, you're the man I need.' He placed a mottled hand tremulously on Atwater's sleeve. 'I've sought you out.'

Atwater felt he knew what was coming. 'I have no system to reveal,' he said, 'cannot be bribed.'

'What the devil are you talking about?'

'Or you,' riposted Atwater neatly.

Beazley's hand quivered more fiercely. 'I told you,' he said. 'It's that swine Horridge, friend of yours, isn't he, the blot on creation? I don't know whether he's after my wife or my daughter.'

'I feel deflated,' said Atwater. 'This is banal. I have troubles myself. Horridge or no Horridge, I have problems to unravel. Things happened last night to perturb me. I could a tale unfold that would do knitted socks stuff on your nut.'

He sipped the champagne cocktail which tasted like every other champagne cocktail he had drunk except those made from cider. Colonel Beazley to his surprise wasn't apparently offended by his words.

'Quite,' he said, 'acquainted with grief too, I dare say, so am I, old fruit. Now let me put it to you as an intermediary, for I won't speak to the swine myself, he can have my wife, welcome to her and best of luck, but my daughter's taboo. Hands off.'

'You mean,' said Atwater, feeling he could stretch a point, 'you would like me to speak to Horridge?'

'And use foul language,' said the Colonel.

'Tell me,' said Atwater, 'about your wife.'

'My wife,' said Colonel Beazley, 'is a basilisk. She is a gorgon. Look at me, Atwater. Beazley the celebrated swine, a figure of the utmost fun. She made me this. Look,' he delved into his wallet and produced a photograph. It showed a young man in uniform. Atwater thought he had never seen a face so totally lacking in character. 'That,' said the Colonel with mist in his voice, 'was me. Was I. Look at me now. I am aware of what I've come to.'

'No one,' said Atwater politely, 'could miss or mistake you now.'

'It is marriage has done it. I make an observation, a mask slides across her face, is it any wonder I froth at the mouth? Listen,' and he dropped his voice to an intimate hiss, 'sex. For thirty years, when I'm at my sexiest, she has a pain. She drives me to the loft with the maid or the native bearer and then reproaches me and swears to deny what she has already denied.'

'How,' said Atwater, 'did your daughter come to be conceived?'

'I slipped in on the blind side on a moonless night.'

Atwater watched the old lunatic with respect.

'Now,' said Beazley, licking his chops, 'she's fallen for Horridge. Now God be thanked who has matched them in this hour. But what happens,' his voice rose in a shriek that caused an Arab millionaire drinking vodka (in defiance of the Prophet) at the other end of the bar hurriedly to check that he was wearing his knife-proof corsets, 'he tears it up by chasing that lubricious bit of skirt, my daughter.'

'Lubricious?'

'Highly lubricious,' he chortled obscenely.

The idea seemed to obsess him. He sat for several minutes on the bar-stool, a rapt expression on his face, for all the world like Mr Toad saying poop-poop.

'Highly lubricious, most awfully lubricious, lubricious.'

Atwater glanced at the clock.

'Don't go,' the Colonel said. 'Don't leave me like this. Don't leave me sunk in gloom.'

'You're very emotional,' Atwater said. 'Where's that stiff upper lip of the English gentleman we read about in the patriotic press?'

'Ah where are the ruins of Rum?' said Colonel Beazley. The thought seemed to console him. 'Come, Atwater, we shall go and see my daughter. But first I must pee.'

'Do you think, sir,' said the barman, 'you could persuade the Colonel to pay his bill?'

'No,' said Atwater honestly.

'It's two hundred and eighty-three pounds.'

Atwater looked at the figure emerging from the loo with a respect that approached veneration. He noticed that the Colonel had changed his moustache. It was now ginger.

It had started to rain.

Atwater felt they had been an unusually long time in the bar, cut off from the world. He eyed Beazley who stood frothing, gently but not at all furtively, at the mouth; Atwater, alerted to his methods, sensed that he was seeking a car to annex.

'Taxi-drivers,' the Colonel said in the tones of one who every Sunday recites the Apostles' Creed, 'are thieves, fit for flogging.'

Beazley was not in fact mad; not quite. Sexual frustration (for he desired his wife), professional disappointment, had stretched his nerves taut. Also he had no money. That accounted for his debts. They were the direct result of his lack of money. This was clear to everybody but his wife and the more unreasonable of his creditors. Recently he had been suffering from insomnia. He was afraid to sleep because of his dreams. He had a nasty feeling he had got mixed up in the last act of Faust. He didn't like it.

An American car, possibly a Fleetwood Cadillac, drew up before the hotel.

Anticipating the porter, the Colonel seized the door handle.

'Take us to Buckingham Palace. There is a royal life at stake.'

Quite soon he told the driver this was a ruse (calculated, he explained kindly, to throw his enemies off the scent) and asked to be taken to an address in Pimlico. The driver, a Negro displaying symptoms of dropsy, obligingly and silently consented.

Atwater began to experience feelings of unwonted awe.

Horridge was in bed with Polly when the doorbell rang. This was unusual. She had for some time refused to share him with her mother.

'It's disgusting,' she had said and begun to cry.

Horridge had told her to stuff all that crap about incest, peasants did it all the time, so it was fucking natural, wasn't it, ecological even, look at cats, and as for tears they made him sick to the gut.

It had taken her a long time before she got back into bed with him though. She was still wondering why she had done it.

'Daddy wants me to marry you,' she sighed.

'Your old man's a fucking lunatic,' he said. 'They're going to put him away, lock him up like. It's a race who gets him first.'

He rolled over on top of her, reminding her why she had changed her mind. As for Polly she was a very pretty girl with blue eyes and many positions. Lots of people fancied her, including her employer, a Tory Member of Parliament with a blue rinse and an Anglo-Catholic conscience. When she thought of Polly she set herself a penance. Polly herself wasn't happy. Life had begun to go wrong when she was twelve and her Exmoor pony had died. Meanwhile one did one's best. Like this.

She said to Horridge,

'I wish . . .'

'Christ . . .'

'What?'

'Christ you're like your bitch of a mother. She's always fucking wishing when she should be fucking fucking.'

'I hate you. Get out of my bed.'

'My bed. How bloody bourgeois, my bed, my . . .'

Colonel Beazley insisted the Negro join them.

'The more,' he said sombrely, 'the merrier.'

The Negro, a dignified man despite his dropsy and diplomatic status, said, 'Just for ten minutes then.'

Atwater said, 'I don't think she can be at home.'

Colonel Beazley began to hammer on the door with his stick. He was a man with a fixed idea. His blood was up. It was clear, Atwater reflected, that neither hobgoblin nor foul fiend (should they be lurking at the turning of the stair) could him dispirit. Eventually the door opened and Horridge looked out.

'What a fucking noise, Fred. Christ, Atwater.'

'Get me a drink,' said Colonel Beazley pushing past him.

Horridge was naked to the waist but had pulled on jeans.

It didn't however seem likely to Atwater that the Colonel would conclude that Horridge had been shaving or sitting under a sun-ray lamp.

'Where's Polly?' said the Colonel waving a gin bottle.

'In the loo,' said Horridge, displaying unprecedented chivalry.

Atwater wondered if he should suggest they all sat down and discussed it like gentlemen, decided it was absurd and said,

'Why don't we all sit down and discuss it like actors? On a chat show perhaps?'

The Colonel said, 'Upon my word, Horridge, are you always to be found under my feet or rather in my beds?'

There was a strange new gentleness in his tone. He spoke like one who had foresuffered all.

'Yesterday my wife, today my daughter. Who tomorrow?'

'Not you, Fred. That's for sure.'

'In my country,' said the Negro, speaking to Atwater in a low and confidential tone, 'we do not like to hear about such things.'

Atwater nodded. He could visualise an article in the dullest and most clotted of the weeklies: 'Emergent Africa; the new Puritanism.'

'We prefer to see them.'

He gave Atwater a card. It read:

Dr Seth Ngunga Ph D
Envoy Extraordinary

Telegraphic address : urgent

Atwater bowed.

'Atwater,' he said.

'Indeed my goodness yes,' said Dr Ngunga breaking into Welsh.

Polly emerged, wearing jeans and a mammoth woolly sweater and looking absurdly young. Any confirmed child-molester would have felt entitled to bring an action for false pretences against her.

Her father got up and kissed her.

'My dear,' he said, 'I come bringing sweetness and light and Mr Atwater too and I find this. You have made an old man very unhappy.'

'Don't cry, Daddy. You know how it makes your mascara run.'

Horridge said, 'Wish I could stay but I've got a bomb to plant.'

'Stop showing off,' said Polly, 'and give Daddy some more gin. The poor lamb's glass is empty.'

Horridge obeyed. Atwater's eyebrows rose. Horridge domesticated.

Much later they sent Dr Ngunga out to buy more gin. He returned with a crate.

Polly came over and sat by Atwater. She said, 'I've heard a lot about you.'

'Oh yes.'

'From Clare and Jeremy.'

'My solicitor.'

'He's crazy about you.'

'Really?'

'So's Clare. She says you're the funniest man she knows.'

Dr Ngunga said, 'And folks say England is finished.'

'The fact is, Horridge,' said Colonel Beazley, 'you and I, we're bound.'

'There's my wife too,' said Horridge.

'My dear boy, I didn't know you were married.'

'May I kiss you, Atwater? Somehow I'd like to kiss you.'

'Certainly, but let's have a spot more gin first.'

'There will always be an England. I had an appointment with the Financial Secretary three hours ago, but do I care? Am I down-hearted? No, sir.'

'As the Governor of North Carolina said to the Governor of South Carolina, my dear Horridge, it's a long time between drinks, said that worthy.'

'I don't know that Clare's right for Jeremy, I mean, I think she's right when she says he should go back to boys, only it seems rather sad.'

'This sceptred sea set in a silvered pearl.'

'Have you met my employer, Mrs Hedge? She's a love, so hard-working. Do you know, she's probably working now. I'm her secretary so I should know.'

'Does she do her own typing?'

'All of it, I simply haven't time, what with things.'

'This worse than teeming womb of royal things
feared for their beards and famous for their girth,
no,
reared by their fyrd and famous for their girth,
stout hearts, like Cortez, wells
of English new-defiled.'

'Colonel, these are mere shibboleths.'

'Well done. Brave lad.'

30

'There are those who say she is England to them.'

'Indeed.'

'I've heard it said.'

'On the tube?'

'And in the greengrocer's.'

'They don't talk about her much in the betting-shops,' said Atwater.

'Well they wouldn't.'

'Sodding Liberals, half of them,' flung in Horridge.

Atwater felt a strange new desire to confide in Polly. He said so.

'Things have been happening on the fringes of my consciousness.'

'Bourgeois eclecticism . . .'

'You reject it?' queried the Colonel.

Polly said, 'Atwater.'

She had quite the nicest most desirable lips he had seen in years. He told her that too.

'And so my wife and my daughter both.'

Dr Ngunga's gaze was fixed on his feet which were very large.

Atwater had once, when eleven, visited a cousin who lived in Highgate. There had been snow on the ground. She had taken him into the cemetery to sledge. Zooming down the hill, quite near Karl Marx now he thought of it, he had experienced an unusually intense sensation. Life was out of control; *ultra vires*; he was possessed.

'If you could pay me, Fred.'

'Is it only the cash nexus can in contradiction unbind?'

'You socks,' said Dr Ngunga, 'you bones, you worse than senseless things.'

'No,' said Horridge, 'but meet me in the Nag's Head *ce soir* and I'll have a proposition.'

'The Nag's Head. Which? When? I know Nags galore, all with heads.'

'Not Nag. Turk. Eightish. Don't waste your talent on Atwater, ducks. He doesn't.'

Horridge's departure from a room was always fraught.

Hopes rose, then sank as he turned back with a final curse, admonition, moan. It tried the nerves. It was like the coming of spring.

Atwater, inured, stared stoically into his gin. Colonel Beazley, less accustomed, changed his moustache, often the sign that a man is not at ease.

II

It was raining, soft insistent Fenland rain, drifting damply down on an already sodden landscape. Polly steered the tiny car nimbly round quite unnecessary corners in the flat and featureless road. Perhaps the corners existed to persuade drivers they were still alive. Atwater huddled miserably in a macintosh, his feet warm from a heater but water trickling down his neck. He was brooding on the rashness of their expedition. They should never have left London.

'Are we lost?' he said . . .

'There's a wind getting up,' he said . . .

'Do you think it will turn to snow?' he said . . .

Polly said, 'Have a sandwich.'

'I expect they're wet through.'

'Give me one all the same.'

Atwater withdrew a small package from a bag, unwrapped it and peeled off soft and clinging bread.

'Egg,' he said, 'and what is called cress. There must be a lot of cress growing in these ditches.'

'If it snows,' she said, 'they all fill up.'

'I can't wait.'

'You do enjoy misery, don't you?'

He took a pull from a flask containing gin and bitters.

'What else is there to do with it?' he said.

Polly sighed. 'I can't speak to my mother.'

'I can't speak to mine either.'

Polly was wary. 'I suppose she's dead?'

'Has been for years.'

'That might make it easier. Mine isn't. Either way, this expedition . . .'

'Your idea.'

'And sweet of you to come.'

'Brave too.'

'Tell me, Atwater, do you think Horridge is dangerous?'

'Sardonic laugh. Horridge is a clown. Like me. Like your father. Like your Mrs Hedge. Like Dr Ngunga. He's a clown, so of course he can be dangerous.'

'What happened to Dr Ngunga?'

'Well, at least you saw him too.'

'Yes, but his departure, it was a bit now you see him now you don't. Are you disgusted I go to bed with Horridge? In all the circumstances.'

'Appalled.'

'It's very hard to explain.'

'Don't try. Take it as read.'

'I can't really explain it to myself. Even without Mummy and all that I'd find it hard.'

'Stop,' said Atwater, 'this world, it all looks terribly real. Not like London. I thought it would be this that was the stage set.'

'If it works out we'll go to the races.'

'Do you mean,' said Atwater, 'it's actually possible to watch real horses run? I'm not sure I should like that. It smacks of profanity.'

'We'll get Clare and Jeremy to come. Jeremy loves racing.'

'Jockeys' silks, I expect.'

They turned off the road in through isolated gates that looked a bit like the remains of Ozymandias. Atwater remarked on this in less literary a way.

'They look as if they've been left out in the rain,' he said.

'Horridge asked me where the cross-bar was. Horridge is up to something. He keeps meeting Daddy in pubs.'

'Their paths are bound to cross from time to time. I'm always meeting a small deaf man with a goatee beard. I don't like it one little bit but when I protest they say it's a free country.'

'Oh that's Denis Drew. He's an actor.'

'He would be.'

'It's not that sort of meeting though. I mean, they arrange it.'

The house came into view. There was little to be said about it. Even the Historic Buildings Commission hadn't had the heart to list it; even Dr Pevsner had been silenced by its numb anonymity. On the other hand there had been no move to knock it down. It appeared now to be guarded by Great Danes. There were four or five lying about on the gravel, too stupid or (conceivably) masochistic, to come in out of the rain.

'Horrid creatures,' said Polly.

'Really,' said Atwater, 'what a refreshing girl you are.'

'Mummy will be inside, I expect.'

It was something, Atwater supposed, that she wasn't lying there on the gravel with the Danes.

The telephone was ringing when they entered a dank hall littered with derelict deck-chairs. Polly picked up the receiver.

'You bitch, I've been calling for an hour and a half.'

'No, Daddy, it's me.'

'Oh you . . . I just wanted to say you were on your way. But you're there, so tell her yourself. Not what I was going to tell her because it's no longer an accurate sit-rep. Tell her you're there. Mind you're polite.'

'You see,' Polly said to Atwater. 'He is sweet.'

It came to Atwater that he had after all a reservation about Polly—beyond of course his permanent reservation about other people, which was simply that they were indeed other people—he must cure her of this habit of calling things sweet.

It wasn't till much later that he found himself pondering the implication of that word 'cure'.

He followed her upstairs. She paused on the first landing, listened and wrinkled her nose.

'Higher up,' she said, 'in the studio.'

'Studio?'

'Didn't you know? Mummy's a sculptor. She was quite well-known once.'

The feeling returned to Atwater that he was in the grip of events moving in a rhythm he couldn't influence. He thought: I have committed myself to action and am foolish enough to have embarked. I am at the mercy of the waves. He fully realised the daring isolation of men who are not in prison. His hand tightened on the gin-flask, over his heart.

The room faced north. Beyond salt-marshes lay the sea. Polly said, 'It's all sea to the Pole.'

Atwater had crossed to the window the better to assimilate the room. It wasn't as bad as he had feared at first. The Great Danes with which this room too appeared to be infested were at least immobile, carved from stone; one, painted as a Harlequin, achieved a certain Fauvish charm. The general effect, the *tout ensemble*, however, repelled. No doubt this accounted in part for the decline in Lady Gertrude's reputation. Once, in the fabled days when artists were to be found in the Fitzroy Tavern, she had been a celebrity; within the coterie at least. Polly had formerly been accustomed to draw her friends' attention to a sketch of her mother by Robert Colquhoun; she had long since desisted. Despite this history it was a tribute to Lady Gertrude's integrity that she had never, even when drunk, claimed to have had occasion to repel or rebuff the advances of a drunken Dylan. These days though she no longer drank. She said as much to Atwater.

'Quite,' he replied.

Instead she consumed huge quantities of bitter Indian tea. She indicated a tea-pot. Atwater declined; courteously. Lady Gertrude lit another Woodbine and seized her chisel.

'I can't stop while the light lasts,' she said, peering out into the gathering crepuscular gloom.

The head of a Dane was emerging from a block of stone. Atwater sat in a desk-chair. He was quite happy. He liked watching people at work. It was even more satisfying when they were botching the job. He felt no vulgar impatience to rush in and put her right.

He said, 'Do you mind if I have some gin? I've brought it with me. I find it supports me.'

'How boring you drunks are,' she said.

She employed her chisel vigorously. With a crack the Dane's head parted company from the parent neck. It rolled across the floor, coming to rest at Atwater's feet. He picked it up.

'Do you do that often?' he asked.

She said to Polly, 'Why have you brought this fellow? He's all I can't stand.'

Atwater sipped gin. He was impervious to such abuse. There had been too many mornings at different periods of his life when he had woken in strange beds and listened to women berating their husbands in the next room. His name had never on such occasions been mentioned in a friendly or admiring spirit.

'I'm worried about Daddy.'

'He's been a lucky man.'

'He's very unhappy. And getting eccentric.'

'Mad as a hatter.'

'Why,' said Polly, 'a hatter? I've often wondered.'

'Roger Crab,' said Atwater.

'What do you mean?'

'He was a hatter. He was mad.'

'You see,' said Polly, 'he's very useful.'

Lady Gertrude ignored this. 'I have something to tell you,' she said. 'I have had a letter from Horridge. He says he will not give me up. Never. It is like the Duke of Windsor.'

Colonel Beazley had come to a decision. This was something that happened to him frequently. Horridge must be eliminated. He saw that his plan would not work. What he had learned from Atwater had convinced him. Horridge could not be brought to the sticking-place. Except by fear. The elimination therefore should not actually take place. The Colonel was becoming confused. A moment ago the situation

37

had been clear. Now some damfool had sewn up the rent veil of the temple. He mopped his brow with a red bandana and poured himself a Pernod. He remembered someone once telling him it was a very cerebral drink. He wished he liked it.

'Beazley, old boy, Beazley, old swine,' he said to himself, 'got to put your thinking-cap on. Tabulate.'

He roared aloud, an anguished bellow that echoed round the cheap hotel.

Horridge was screwing again. This time his victim was a little shopkeeper's large assistant in Golder's Green.

'Oooh,' she said, 'aaah. Eeeh.'

'You have nothing to lose but your chains,' said Horridge between strokes.

The young man whose features were less Jewish than Atwater had imagined but who would nevertheless have had a good chance of landing a bit-part in a film of the Crucifixion or the Stoning of Stephen, had approached Clare and Jeremy, crab-like, as they sat in the Queen's Elm, in the corner beside the partition between the bars.

'I'm a friend of Atwater's,' he said.

Jeremy gobbled pinkly and waved a pudgy hand.

'I'm glad to hear it,' said the young man. 'That goes for me too. What are you . . .?' The word hovered on his lips, but he fought it back and sat down. 'I'm a novelist,' he said.

'You could still buy us a drink,' thought Clare, but the young man carried such a weight of oppression around with him that she left the words unsaid. She was actually a bit surprised to have found herself thinking them.

'I'm a bit worried about Atwater,' the young man said, 'that's why I've well . . . impo . . . self on you actually.'

'Oh,' said Jeremy, 'I say, I say, we're all absolutely arid. Can't have that. What's yours?'

'Brandy and ginger.'

'The fact is,' said the novelist, not waiting for Jeremy to return, 'Atwater's behaving very strangely. Something's up. Do you know he's left London.'

Clare hated him. She wasn't going to tell him anything, not even what he knew already.

'Now,' said the novelist, placing a scaly hand on the table, letting it creep raggedly across its surface and hover like some loathsome and venomous insect over her knee, 'Atwater can't do this. It's all wrong. He's a character in my novel, you know, and this sort of behaviour disrupts the rhythm. I may have to dispose of him.'

Clare felt the hair rising on the back of her neck. It was absurd because the man was mad. It was not absurd because after all the man was mad.

'Here we are. One brandy and ginger for you, sir, and a gin and tonic for Clarici and Harry Pinkers for me.'

'I have plans for you too,' the novelist said. 'I've been watching you all.'

The wind howled past the Chinese restaurants and blew damp pages of the *Evening Standard* swirling against the doors of Finch's. The bar was emptier than usual. You could see across it. It was a night to keep people even in bed-sitters. There were regulars missing though the woman in the flowered hat who was reputed to have distinguished herself on the Republican side in the Spanish War—'*la Pasionaria* of the Fulham Road' as some called her—was in her usual place.

Richie surveyed the dwindled crowd morosely. 'Goddam Pommy sheep,' he said or snarled, 'night like this and they settle with Frosties in front of the telly. Makes you sick, Jerry. Even Atwater's not here. Can you beat it?'

'Gone to the country.'

'Atwater? That's crazy. He's in jug again.'

'No, sir, he's gone off with a girl, had it on the very best authority.'

'Atwater with a sheila?'
'Good authority it was.'
'Christ, man, the whole globe's going coot.'

'I thought novelists were supposed to invent,' said Clare.
Her cheeks were pink.
The young man looked at her.
'Invent,' he said.
Clearly words failed him; he was flummoxed.

'No,' Horridge said, 'I am married already.'
'Stuff it then. You can stuff it then.'

It was no good. Whoever said that about Pernod was a
liar. Or a fool. There were always alternatives. He might as
well have been drinking gin. He began to do so.

Atwater removed the dog's head from his lap. The gesture
was becoming almost automatic. One after another the brutes
approached. He understood how Macbeth must have felt
when the hags showed him the unending line of Banquo's
heirs. He waited impatiently for the crack of doom.

'That true, man, what the man said?'
'Christ it's Aloysius, old cobber, Aloysius old sport. Yeah,
it's true, strange isn't it, and he doesn't have to pay alimony, you know, not a bleeding cent.'
'I tell you often, Richie man, what to do with them wives
of yours, but you no listen to old Aloysius. You don' wan' to
pay them no alimony, you wan' to sell them, man.'
'No takers, bloody fools all dead.'

'You give Aloysius twenty per cent, man, commission, and I find you takers, you bet.'

Clare kicked Jeremy under the table.

The novelist said, 'It's all to do with patterns, tracing the arabesques of life.'

They had eaten in silence. Atwater prodded the rice pudding with his fork. It reminded him of prison. He hadn't seen it elsewhere since prep-school. Those, in a curious sense, were the days. Rice pudding and semolina; food for the innocent. Polly was near crying. He hoped she wouldn't.

'I still don't understand why you have come. Nothing will persuade me. Your father has driven me to it. Have you ever thought what it's been like, all these years. Look out there,' she drew back the curtain and revealed the night. 'Out there, the long beach and the empty sea. Marriage.'

Atwater was bored. 'Horridge has a wife,' he said. 'She's called Harriet. The last time I saw her . . .' He sipped gin.

'You have known Horridge a long time?'

Lady Gertrude looked directly at Atwater. Her eyes were a hard pale-blue; 'arctic' was the word that came to mind.

'We were boys together,' he replied. 'We paddled in the burn.'

'I feel Horridge is only now coming into his prime. He burns with a strange dark fire.'

'He has very peculiar hair,' Polly said, 'what there is of it, that is.'

'It has quality.'

'Perhaps you should both meet Harriet. Again perhaps not.'

'I see nothing in it . . . nothing to be . . .'

'She lives all day in a dressing-gown, I'm told.'

'That would not do at all for Horridge. He demands . . .'

'He did for her.'

'You've got some very strange ideas about Horridge, Mummy. I like what he does in bed, I think he's foul otherwise.'

'That's frank,' Atwater said; it was the modern touch.

'Actually he's pretty foul there too, but exciting.'

'You can bleeding well get out then and go back to her,' said the girl throwing a sweat-stained T-shirt (motto: How can We Lose when we're so Sincere) in Horridge's face. 'Bleeding cheek, that's what. I'd get my husband to sort you, duff you up like. He's a West Indian.'

'What?' cried Horridge, stimulated and leaping back beside her.

'Only I can't, see, 'cos he's in the bleeding nick, i'n't he?'

Colonel Beazley had started to draw. His design was intricate. It was copied from the Cabbala. This alarmed him. He had always said,

'Mark my words, if I come to that, I'm finished. Beazley for the knackers, it'll be.'

No one had contradicted him.

Now, in the cheap hotel with the lemon walls, the chipped mirror, the sagging mattress and the ever present aroma of dry rot (or was it moral decay?) he sat precariously at a table designed with no purpose in mind, his hand moving relentlessly, involuntarily, over sheet after sheet of paper, tracing a design by means of which he might yet confound his enemies.

He got it all wrong too.

Jeremy sat on the edge of the bed and said, 'Shall I join you?'

'I didn't like that man. I don't know why you wanted to keep buying him drinks. He's trying to do something to Atwater. All that about him being a character in his novel. I didn't like it. It was sinister.'

'Sinister? Bit plastered, I thought.'

He sighed with an autumn melancholy.

'Oh, Clarici, I don't know what I could do without you, I'm so miserable.'

'Poor Jeremy . . . have you . . . you know . . . tried?'

The pink cheeks incarnadined like sunset in the Rockies.

'Oh you don't want to know about that.'

'Yes, I do.'

'You can't.'

'Can.'

'It's not very, it's not nice . . .'

'Tell you what, get in here with me and tell me here. Cosy.'

Lady Gertrude had gone to bed escorted by the troupe of Danes.

'They howl otherwise.'

'Then take them.'

'Like banshees.'

'Or demon lovers.'

'It was the woman.'

'What?'

'Who howled. Not the demon lover. He, poor chap, was silent. Overwhelmed, I dare say.'

Polly came over and sat at Atwater's feet.

'What's going to happen?' she said.

Atwater, ignorant, was silent.

'Horridge and Mummy, it's silly. What does he see in her?'

'You don't understand Horridge,' Atwater said. He swallowed gin. 'Horridge has no interest in sensuality. That doesn't arouse him.'

Atwater was in a strange mood, he felt prophetic. The country air, perhaps, or the effect of the country air when laced with gin. Stranger still he felt a desire to communicate. A voice warned him of the dangers but he declined to hear it. He put his hand on Polly's head. It was the first time in

43

three years he had, unprompted, of his own accord, touched another.

'Horridge,' he said, 'is attracted by power. That's what arouses him. He feels himself to be a destructive force. He likes to complicate people's lives and then tear them apart. That is Horridge. It's political of course. All sex is politics ultimately, I've heard him say that and I see what he means. What more *petit bourgeois* than a married couple in a semi; of course sex fixes your political attitudes and, in the way you always get things coming and going, is at the same time, the expression of them. Horridge gets quite lyrical about it.'

'So he gets in and stirs up shit,' Polly said. 'I've felt it. I couldn't have found the words but that's what I've felt.'

'It's the will in action,' Atwater said, 'it always is. Would you like to sleep with me?'

Polly turned round like an unusually flexible small animal and kissed him.

'No,' she said.

'Why not?' asked Atwater relieved.

'Because I'm sleeping with Horridge, bloody as he is, and I don't think of myself as a whore. That's my politics.'

'You're wrong, you know, about what your father wants,' Atwater said. 'He doesn't want you to marry Horridge.'

Actually Atwater was unsure about this; he'd only the Colonel's word for it and it was more than somewhat possible that, in this instance at least, Colonel Beazley had intended the exact opposite of what he said.

'Oh good, I needn't feel guilty.'

'What about?'

'Well, I'm not going to marry Horridge, am I?'

'Oh.'

'Obviously not . . . why did you ask me to sleep with you?'

'It just occurred to me.'

'Horridge said you didn't.'

'Not often.'

'Why not, if you don't mind my asking?'

'Of course I don't.'

'Well, then . . . I feel I'm getting to know you, Atwater.'

Atwater was alarmed, yet attracted. He was aware of something that had long been absent from his life. He had felt the same temptation with Clare in the Indian restaurant; more weakly. Atwater had never liked beaches, but, once, aged eighteen, he had found himself on one in Dorset with several pretty girls wearing bikinis (then a relatively new and even daring garb) and school-friends in bathing-trunks. For two hours he had sat in regulation school grey flannel trousers, grey Viyella shirt, grey socks and brown brogues. He had read Aldous Huxley—*Those Barren Leaves* perhaps—while they cavorted around him, chasing each other into the water, throwing a ball about, diving from the rocks, or, most seductive of all, lazing beside him, soaking up the sun, rubbing sun-tan oil into soft pinking flesh or rippling muscles. One girl, her name was Caroline—how many were Caroline in those far-off innocent 'fifties when the first juke-boxes played Johnny Ray's 'It was a night, it really was such a night' and Frankie Laine called lonesomely for an Answer from the Lord Above—lay before him, as the sun passed the meridian, in the arms of his friend Robin, now a paunchy management consultant with greying hair and a house in Chiswick. Then still intertwined with Robin, she had thrust the top half of her body upward, short, black, sand-streaked hair swinging, and young, assertive breasts, and, a cigarette in her mouth, had asked for a light, darling Ru, which no one had ever called him before or since. It had been very hard to concentrate on Mr Huxley after that. She had looked over the cigarette, into him, as he lit it for her. A few weeks later, a propos of nothing, quite out of the blue, a married woman, in whom he had no interest, had told him that was the sign, the indelible mark, of a flirt, to look in your eyes as you lit her cigarette. The image of Caroline, as of something missed, had often returned to him in dark and steamy nights. She had married very young;

45

in the 'fifties one of her urgence turned more naturally to early marriage and subsequent adultery than to what they later began to call a free life style. She could be a grandmother now; just.

Polly said, 'So, Atwater, do you believe . . . what do you believe in?'

'Nothing.'

Polly drew back her head. A gust of wind from the sea made the shutters rattle.

'It's bloody of me,' said Jeremy, 'and bloody for you. Oh why am I such a shit?'

'There, there,' Clare said. She sat up in bed and stroked his hair. It was coarse and springy, like an Irish Terrier's.

He said, 'But what is one to do? If my uncle knew about it, well . . .'

'The Shropshire clients, you mean. . . ?'

'Wouldn't like it.'

'Perhaps you haven't found the right boy yet. You never know, a Shropshire lad maybe.'

'Don't laugh. It's not that. It's just that when I'm actually on the job, it seems awfully silly. I feel such a fool.'

'And with me?' she couldn't help asking. He began to cry again. There is that side to sex, Clare thought, you've just got to accept it. Atwater had quoted something to her; position ridiculous, pleasure momentary and expense damnable. All quite, quite true. It didn't alter the fact that she was feeling awfully randy now. Her fingers began to play softly on Jeremy's groin.

Afterwards he said, 'Shall we go racing on Saturday?'

'Where?'

'Kempton.'

'We could take Atwater and Polly.'

'What a brilliant . . . do them good.'

'Us too. All the good in the world.'

'Glad that's settled.'

Jeremy lay back. A few minutes later he began to snore. Clare got up, made herself a cup of coffee, put a Count Basie record on rather loudly, did some yoga exercises, drank more Nescafé and eventually took a downie through and curled up in it on the bathroom floor. Even with the door shut she couldn't escape the snores. She fell asleep wondering if anyone had ever done anything on the psychological effect of snoring on the sex-drive. She must ask Atwater.

It had come out. He was one step forward. He needed the co-operation of someone with Polly's weal at heart. He braved himself. At last he began to dress, hesitating longer than usual over his choice of moustache.

Dr Ngunga waited in a dark alley. Sometimes he felt he was getting too old for these furtive assignations. He wriggled his toes inside his shoes inside his goloshes. To pass the time he pondered on his own, his unique distinction. Perhaps this would at last lead to that All Souls fellowship of which he had in the past been so unfairly deprived.

'I have done the State some service,' he murmured.

Orphanages all over the southern suburbs of his native capital attested to this.

'Death to the French,' said a voice.

'And with thy spirit,' replied Ngunga.

Another blunder.

'Atwater,' said the voice, 'is the key. He must be picked.'

'Up or off?'

He was practising this brand of facetious wit for the High Table. It was greatly in demand there.

'Atwater,' he said. 'The plot thickens.'

In the elegant mews flat where all was painted white and the carpets were alternately dove-grey and rose-pink, two lights still shone. One was never extinguished. It was Mrs

47

Hedge's private chapel, so private that it had only once been photographed for a Sunday newspaper colour supplement.

Mrs Hedge knelt before the altar, or what would have been the altar had the chapel in fact been consecrated. She was rapt in prayer. She wore a sackcloth twin-set and skirt, as recommended by *Vogue* the previous Lent, choicest penitential garments. They had never quite caught on.

Her gaze was fixed on the altar-piece, a whimsical oil, showing the Virgin addressing the Conservative Women's League. The Mother of God wore a mauve toque on her head.

'I have erred and strayed from thy ways,' said Mrs Hedge, incompletely convinced. Her problem was how to combine her profound conviction of inherent righteousness with a keen sense of sin. It had brought her close to suicide as a child. On the advice of a psychiatrist in Leighton Buzzard she had tried to exorcise her awareness of sin by entering politics. Her psychiatrist had told her it would 'obviate the guilt syndrome'.

That was before she met Polly.

In the next room her husband, the television closed down, played Scrabble, right hand against left.

Mrs Hedge's lips moved. In prayer her accent lost none of its refined cultivation. She addressed the Almighty with the same indulgent candour with which she charmed Tory voters.

'I shall not rest,' she said, 'till I have established our relationship on a truer, more lasting basis. Self-interest cannot be allowed to roam untrammelled but neither can it be permitted in this day and age, even at this moment in time, to be smothered by the outworn shibboleths of a male-dominated society.'

'Mark my words,' she had told a Women's Rotary Wheel session, 'women are God's answer to Socialism.'

That had made them sit up in the Carlton Club.

Atwater and Polly were wandering on the beach. They had evaded even truant Danes.

'There's no point,' she said, 'staying. Mummy lives now

in a world of her own peopled only by Horridge. How I'm beginning to hate the sound of his name . . . what I don't see is what he sees in her.'

Atwater looked out over the sea which was now quite calm. The rain had stopped, the clouds were clearing and becoming wispy. A moon, probably the moon now he came to think of it, was revealed. Everything was quiet, even the sea-gulls, except Polly still babbling of Horridge. He realised he endorsed her sentiments. Horridge was becoming a bit of a bore.

'Polly,' he said, 'we could put an embargo on Horridge talk.'

'I'm sure I don't want to talk about him. I just wish I knew why he went for Mummy. I mean, can you see them in bed?'

'Only too easily,' shuddered Atwater.

It was always only too easily; no combination so absurd that two people would not be found to enact it.

Mr Hedge didn't recognise Colonel Beazley when he opened the door to him.

'I'm the Chairman of your wife's Constituency Association,' the Colonel boomed, letting a good part of the citizenry of Westminster into the secret.

'At this time of night?'

'Always. Like the Windmill I never close. May I see your wife, if,' he added politely for it had seemed a harsh thing to say, 'she is indeed your wife?'

'Certainly she is.'

'Brave lad. I have an old soldier's admiration for courage.'

'She is in the chapel.'

'Alone?'

'Except for the Pekingese.'

'And the Almighty.'

'Of course.'

'We must never forget him. Would you call yourself a religious man?'

'No,' said Mr Hedge.

He sighed. The introduction of religion into his marriage had distressed him. If it was now going to form part of his conversation with total strangers, it would be a bit thick. He couldn't put it more strongly, having a limited vocabulary.

'Listen,' said Colonel Beazley, 'never mind that. Would you call yourself a drinking man?'

'I'm fond of a light ale with my supper and a gin and tonic on Saturday evenings.'

'A man after my own heart,' said the Colonel. 'Would it be possible, d'you think, while your lady wife' (he was sure that struck the right note) 'is finishing her wee prayer, for me to wet my whistle?'

'Wet your whistle?'

'Yes, have a snifter, a snoggin, a quick one, splice the mainbrace. Good God, man, do you want me to throw the whole of *Roget's Thesaurus* at you? Can I, in plain English, have a spot of gin?'

'Right ho, my name's Mervyn, by the way. Do you know, I'm not sure I caught your name?'

'Beazley,' the Colonel smirked, 'pretty well-known name in some quarters, though I say it myself.'

'Well, Colonel Beazley, cheers. You know, drinking gin at three o'clock in the morning, that's something I've never done.'

Colonel Beazley remembered that he sometimes wore an Old Harrovian tie in time to check his surprise.

'You're too young,' he said, 'to have known the war.'

'Matter of fact, I was a major. In Korea.'

'Korea,' said the Colonel acting instinctively on an old device; when flummoxed, repeat the last speaker's words, derisively.

Sad rank, anyway, major.

Lady Gertrude sat at her writing-desk.

'Where,' she wrote, 'is the rose without the thorn? Polly's arrival made me see the miracle of our love. You have awakened me. You are indeed my Prince.'

Her pen moved fluently over the paper; much more in the same vein.

The Collected Works of Barbara Cartland stood arrayed, a mighty army, on her bookshelves.

She kept the door of this room locked.

Dr Ngunga mistrusted the staircase. These West Indians were degenerate and corrupt; mongrel stock. He had written a paper on the subject; well received at the Brod Sociology Biennale. It was typical that they should live south of the river. He had realised from the first this was an error to be avoided.

His guide, a painfully effeminate Jamaican, said, 'Hush-a-bye baby doc, staircase not so okey-dokey here. Ol' bitch jus' lets the place go to rack an' ruin, what can you expect, bo', from a dyke auntie?'

He patted Dr Ngunga tenderly on the top of the head. The doctor winced. These liberties must, he realised, be endured. For the moment his free will was curtailed.

The Jamaican giggled. 'Call me Wilson,' he said, 'it's all the same to me.'

Dr Ngunga frowned darkly. Perhaps it would have been better years ago to commit himself either to the KGB or All Souls. One or the other. Was he, like many another man of various genius, the second Duke of Buckingham or Wyndham Lewis, for example, to aim at many marks and hit none? Perish the thought.

'Is Horridge actually here?' he said.

'That man jus' makes me grope with nerves.'

He scratched on the door. It swung open.

Horridge said, 'It's a poker game see, you've come here for a poker game.'

'Poker,' giggled the young Jamaican who called himself Wilson, 'that's a real man's game.'

'Take your money soon as look at you.'

'Say, why . . .'

'Sooner, fact, now I do look at you.'

'Why say now, baby . . .'

'Spread the cards.'

Dr Ngunga sat heavily. 'This poker,' he said, 'I understand, a good device, but these children, this obvious catamite . . .'

'Say now, doc . . .'

'Brought you here . . .'

'In my country, in my youth, well I could not say, now
that I observe there is a lady present.'

'Is no lady, is my wife.'

'Ho, ho, ho.'

'He say, is no lady, is his wife.'

'Tha's a lie, is Garnet's.'

'Garnet's doin' bird.'

'So?'

'So, man, got no use for a wife, ain't got no use man.'

Dr Ngunga began to wonder why he had come. Sometimes
he all but despaired of the wisdom of his chiefs. He gazed
at Horridge in desperation.

'Got some information.'

Gin was beginning to interfere with Colonel Beazley's
articulation.

'Information.'

'Yes,' said Mr Hedge gloomily.

He supposed it was better than questions or complaints.
They were the bottom. He would never get to bed. Early in
their marriage his wife had laid it down that it was brutal for
a husband to go to bed first. It was his duty to lock up. And
take the dog out. These were things that shouldn't be demanded of a woman.

'I can't interrupt her in the chapel,' he said. 'It's like Blue
Books and White Papers, sacred, you know.'

'God,' said the Colonel decisively, 'can wait. He is after all
outside time. A thousand ages in his sight are but an evening
gone. Or so they tell us. Therefore . . .'

'It's not God, it's Rosemary. Are you married, Colonel?'

Mr Hedge was not an imaginative man. He was also modest. He had grown accustomed to being ignored, had fallen into the habit of speaking confident that no one was listening; he might almost have been a back-bencher. He was all the more alarmed therefore to see how his innocent question afflicted the Colonel.

Sympathetically he re-filled the Colonel's glass though he couldn't but feel that the old fellow had had a drop too much already. In the circumstances, if he had wife trouble, it was understandable.

Polly stopped the car in a lay-by.

'Do you ever feel, Atwater, that it's all quite quite pointless?'

'It's been my inmost conviction all my life.'

'Then why?'

She felt the shrug of his shoulders.

'The trouble is,' she said, 'that though it's that, it's somehow awfully real too. I mean, look at Daddy.'

'Yes.'

Atwater employed the slightly guarded tone he judged expedient. Polly had tender feelings for the old lunatic, the result, doubtless, of being his daughter.

'What I feel about Daddy is that he went wrong somewhere.'

Atwater found it easy to assent.

'Somewhere awfully important. Do you know, one day, he said to me, looking awfully lost, poor lamb, and almost spilling his gin, "it came to me in the desert that everything I'd been brought up to believe in made no sense at all". I didn't ask him what he meant. I didn't need to.'

'No,' said Atwater, 'one sees it only too clearly. Obligation, service, the rigid lip, all gone. The prophets always found illumination in the desert. It's where they went in search of truth. Jehovah spoke to them there. Inconvenient, but one sees his point. No distractions, nothing to do but listen. Appalling if one thinks of it.'

53

'It was Rommel took Daddy there.'

'God moves in a mysterious way. The working of Providence, very odd.'

'And so poor Daddy was broken. Like a machine running free.'

'Off the rails.'

'Without a goal.'

'Rotten for him.'

'Nothing to do but snatch the moment.'

Polly sighed. She turned round and kissed Atwater. Her tongue pressed against his, began to explore his mouth. He gasped.

There was, she was certain, an aura round her. All had been promised. She awaited delivery. It was therefore disconcerting to discover her constituency chairman and not his daughter.

'I have come to you,' he said, 'instead of the police.'

Mrs Hedge was alarmed. What could the girl have said?

Colonel Beazley was finding it more difficult than he had envisaged.

'You may have heard of one Horridge,' he snuffled eventually.

'Horridge?'

Her tone was ministerial; it suggested that she required notice of that question.

'Polly,' she said carefully, testing the ground, 'is a delightful girl.'

'Lubricious.'

'Really?'

'Highly lubricious.'

'Always liked her,' said Mr Hedge rashly. The sort of warm cuddly thing a man wanted to come home to after a hard day's selling. He had often thought so; this was the nearest he had come to saying it. He wondered what lubricious meant. It might be just what he needed.

'Lubricious, lubricious, but,' said the Colonel collecting

himself, 'that's not exactly the point. Though it ties up. Part of the woof. The great Web as old Marcus Aurelius liked to put it.'

Mrs Hedge, still wary, was beginning to feel irritated also. Blackmailers should come to the point. It was infuriating when they displayed eel-like evasiveness proper to Labour ministers.

'This Horridge,' said the Colonel, 'more gin, more gin for the old sod please. You see it goes against my training. And my nature. Never bandy a lady's name.'

'Horridge is a lady?'

'No.'

The negative was thunderous. Alarming. Mr Hedge thrust the gin into the trembling hands. This fellow might break something. He supposed these constituency chairmen were all the same. Power-mad. Colonels too. They ought to try selling dog food for a bit.

'No.' The Colonel shook his head. 'But there are ladies in the offing. Involved in the case.'

'I see.'

Actually Mrs Hedge was finding the fog thicker.

Aloysius, Atwater's betting-shop disciple, was looking for the action. He was also swaying amiably. That Richie man, he was a real devil. Him and his women. There was money there for ol' Aloysius, right enough, sure thing, bo', you bet. Meanwhile a li'l poker, round Benny's place, settle the stomach. A tolerant man, Aloysius, nothing 'gainst white men or nancy-boys. Jus' a laugh a minute for ol' Aloysius.

Atwater now, he needed taking care of.

Aloysius had a plan to become his valet. He'd recently spent an evening watching television and seen a programme about a young man with a valet. That was the life, valeting; he wondered how much it would cost.

Polly said to Atwater, 'I'm not going to ask you back, not yet anyway. I have to think. It's all complicated.'

55

'The workings of the flesh leave the working of the spirit nowhere as a mystery. Left standing at the post. Or so it often seems. At other times of course quite the reverse. All part of life's great maze as you might say if you were drunker than I seem to be. It's why I've been wary of both.'

'You ought to speak to Daddy about it.'

Atwater sighed, recovered himself.

'Actually,' he said, 'your father is one of the few who might understand my meaning.'

'Are you still in Jermyn Street?'

'Certainly.'

'You are funny, Atwater. Don't you find it strange there?'

'It's convenient and they ask no questions. Besides you often meet people you know there. It's where I met your father.'

'But not having a home?'

'It is like the rocks for the conies. I'm better off than the Son of Man.'

'I don't think I know him.'

'Steer clear, it gets tough, that knowledge.'

'It annoys Mrs Hedge, Rosemary I call her now. She doesn't like hearing him called that. She's hot on the Virgin of course.'

'Hot on her?'

'Very. She says she shows us the path.'

'I see.'

The little car edged into Jermyn Street. A thin dawn was breaking blankly.

'Makes the street look very bald, wouldn't you say?' Atwater remarked.

'I love the dawn.'

'Beginnings . . .'

'If you could arrange life so as to be up and about at the times you like . . .'

'Make things jerky . . .'

'But fun . . . where shall I see you, when?'

'Tonight, the Queen's Elm.'

'All right, but I'm not sure I like pubs.'

56

'Don't say such things, even think them . . .'

He uncoiled from the car, inclined towards her and brushed her cheek. She smelt of the morning.

'It's agreed then,' the Colonel said, 'you'll alert Special Branch. Have friends there myself of course, but in the what-d'you-call-'ems better coming from you. Roger?'

Mr Hedge looked at his wife wonderingly. Of course, politics brought you into contact with all sorts, he understood that, but surely there were limits.

'You say Polly knows this Horridge,' she remarked in a casually steel voice that reminded her husband of the time in the early days of their marriage when he had engaged a secretary sufficiently attractive to attract the odd wolf-whistle in a badly lit alley in Widnes, Wigan or Cowden-beath, in November, the weather being foggy; that had been before his bankruptcy, of course.

'They are like this.' Colonel Beazley tried to cross his fingers but missed.

'Quite so.'

'Ugandan affairs.'

'Ugandan?'

'*Veramente.*'

'I shall speak to Polly. It is monstrous, a girl of her calibre . . . and you are quite certain . . .'

'KGB. Couldn't be anything else.'

'I have a contact in the CIA, a most reliable man, we could check there.'

The Colonel sighed . . . 'Worse than NBG . . .'

'How can you . . . ?'

'American and . . . their record suggests . . .'

'What?'

'The whole organisation is a KGB front.'

Aloysius was wearing a green plastic eye-shade and a large cigar. The pile of chips before him had been growing for two hours. He was beginning to believe that very soon he could afford to hire Atwater as employer.

And now Wilson was trying to beat his four aces with a royal straight flush.

'In my mathematics,' said Aloysius from the corner of his mouth that didn't hold the cigar, 'that just ain't on, baby.'

'Mighty strange pack this,' giggled Milson, extending his slim-fingered hand towards the pile of chips.

'Well,' interposed Dr Ngunga, 'we don't want trouble.'

'Ho, he, ho, hear what the man say, Nicky?'

'Sure, I hear, Bimbo, don' wan' trouble, why you think we come here man?'

'Charity, baby,' Aloysius said, 'is somethin' I'm fresh out of.'

Horridge plucked Dr Ngunga by the sleeve. The good doctor, anxious to act as a peacemaker, tried to brush him off.

'Last time I heard weren't no more but four aces in a deck.'

'Nobody tell you 'bout the terrible inflation this country's sufferin', Aloysius baby.'

'Come on,' said Horridge. Rare tact prevented him from adding 'you fat old baboon'.

'A pity,' said Dr Ngunga, 'when a game between gentlemen . . .'

'It'll go on for hours,' Horridge said. 'I've been waiting for something like this.'

He had at last lured the doctor to the window.

'These West Indians, mongrel stock, given to violence, knives I shouldn't wonder.'

'They'll be still more distracted then. Have you got the stuff?'

Dr Ngunga cleared a diplomatic throat.

'There has been, it appears, a technical maladjustment. A certain degree of what you might call misprision; in short, a cock-up.'

'There has, has there? I need it fast. What gives?'

Horridge in emergency frequently retreated to the security of nineteen-forties diction.

'The hitch (or cock-up) is, according to my principals, the responsibility of one, Atwater. I believe we both know the gentleman.'

'Atwater?'

'It surprises you?'

Horridge pushed his glasses up his nose.

'I confess,' Dr Ngunga sighed, 'it staggered me. I do not conceal it. I am ashamed of my lack of perspicuity, but not to confess it. And yet, consider: how little we know each other, no man is an islander, each of us is continental, part of life's mainstream.'

There came a shrill screech of pain from the table.

'Next time,' said Aloysius, 'I put the knife through your dirty thievin' hand, baby, then maybe you learn yourself to count, sure thing.'

'There can be no doubt, I think. Beneath that ineffectual exterior lurks a brain. Atwater is an agent.'

'This is bloody ridiculous,' said Horridge.

'That,' smiled the doctor, 'is doubtless what you are meant to think. Recall the Scarlet Pimpernel, who would have thought it of him?'

Horridge shook his head.

'I have to warn you, it will be dangerous, my Horridge, if we attempt individual action. My principals, to say nothing of my principles,' he tittered wittily, 'would deplore such deviationism.'

Atwater had always been a slow waker; it was one of the things which disqualified him from work.

'Give me the luxury of three hours to wake in,' he often said.

The opportunity of this, while watching others' more urgent risings and departures, was one of the pleasures of life in the Turkish Baths that he would be loath to quit. Another, powerful to one with his experience of life in bed-sitters in

Pimlico, West Kensington and Shepherd's Bush, was the constant supply of hot water.

His tea was ready when he returned from his bath.

'Got anything good the day, Mr Atwater?' Mac snuffled.

'Not had a chance yet to study the form.'

'There was a loony here asking for ye.'

'A loony?'

'Aye, nobbut a wee bit boy. They wadna let him in. Shall I tak this suit to the pressing for ye? The ither' yin'll be ready. T'at'll gie ye an opportunity to study the form. Och the polis forbye was asking for ye too.'

'Polis? Polis? Police?'

'Aye, the boys in blue. But Joey sent them aff wi' a flea in the lug. We've enough trouble here wi'oot the likes of youz, he tellt them.'

'I should think so too. Did he give them the chance to say what they wanted with me?'

'Na, na, no' Joey, he's ower fly. Weel weel, I'll awa' to the pressing.'

Atwater was irritated to find his enjoyment of his tea and scrutiny of the racing page disturbed by the mention of the police. Difficult to persuade himself that they had made a mistake, were searching for some other of the same name. Atwater left such comforts to those with less than the mean of paranoia. What was worrying was precisely his certainty that he had committed no crime. That meant that the police wanted him for what he was, not for anything he had done. He expounded this view to Richie two hours later in the Queen's Elm.

'Still,' said Richie, 'can't be after you for alimony, now, can they? Ain't never been married, have you, now? So that's sure enough.'

'What you don't understand,' said Atwater speaking with rare patience for he remembered that the other was Australian, 'is that it might be precisely that. If the police are after you for something you have done, or left undone when you ought to have done it, then that's clear enough. You know where you are. My case is quite the reverse. Because they have nothing on me, they have absolutely anything on me. It's the person, not the act, they are proceeding against.'

'Still, like I said, you don't have some sheila trying to screw the balls off you.'

'That would at least be a specific problem.'

'Let's have another jar.'

'You drink too much, both of you, but it's working out, I'll say that, it's working out.'

It was the putatively Jewish soi-disant novelist.

'Who the fuck do you think you're talking to?'

'I doubt,' Atwater remarked, 'whether he is capable of answering you. Not held like that.'

The barman, politely, asked Richie to desist.

'Not that he isn't asking for it. He's always annoying the clientele.'

'Why don't you eject him?' Atwater asked.

'Or throw him out?'

'Can't . . . 'E's one of the boss's literary friends, licensed.'

'It should be revoked. No,' Atwater said, 'I will not buy you a drink.'

'I told you,' said the novelist, 'your character's deteriorating. Wait till the fifth act. As for this barbarian,' he rubbed his throat, 'I'll fix him.'

'You know something? I'd say this guy was coot, real coot.'

Polly woke up in tears. This had never happened to her before and she couldn't understand it. She made herself a cup of coffee and had a hot bath and found she was crying again.

'It's something physical,' she said, 'it must be.'

But she felt an emptiness that made her doubt her diagnosis.

The telephone rang.

'Clare here, can we come round and see you darling?'

'Super, you and Jeremy, yes?'

'So glad we've got you, why aren't you working though?'

'Well, Mrs Hedge and me, we work in spasms. She only needs me when we're saving the country.'

'Have you seen Atwater?'

'He came with me to Mummy's.'

'Did he?'

'But, Clare, why aren't you working? You don't have the country to take a day off from saving?'

'Oh we are working, Jeremy and me, we're investigating.'

'Do solicitors investigate? In person?'

'They're not very good at it. We'll be right round.'

'Lovely, oh I love the telephone, it's a shame you can't take it with you, bye for now, *ciao* . . .'

But she held the receiver for some minutes after she heard Clare replace it, listening to its hum. There was a thin drizzle in the street and the church clock said half past four.

Atwater hadn't backed a winner. His judgment was impaired. Also, because of the police, he hadn't gone to his usual betting-shop. Earlier, he had insisted to Richie that they leave the Queen's Elm and go to another pub where he wasn't known.

'Do they exist?'

There was something jarring and inherently unsatisfactory about Australian laughter; it was the laughter of people too eager to assure you they had seen the joke.

Now he left the betting-shop dissatisfied. The rain fell soft and grey. It lay like mist on his coat. The street lamps shone orange. It came to Atwater that he must change his way of life. Sooner or later the police would get into the Turkish Baths. They were like conscience, could only be denied so long. Atwater looked behind him. The street was empty. Then a pariah dog emerged from the shadows and snuffled in the gutter. Atwater felt a shaft of penetrating cold. He came to a corner and bought an *Evening Standard* from a man with no nose. This, since Atwater had often bought a paper from him and even met him in bars, was less alarming than if he had, suddenly, had one. Atwater put the paper in his pocket without glancing at it and realised at last where he was going.

He hadn't been to the Snakes-and-Ladder Club for two or three years but had no doubt of finding it open. He descended the narrow corkscrew stair past the posters advertising Ivor Novello musicals and Bea Lillie at the Café·de Paris, put his eye to the spy-hole, realised this was foolish since unlike those in prisons this was constructed to enable those within to see out, and rang the bell.

The shutter clicked open. He felt himself surveyed; just like the gaol now or, some would say, God. The door edged open.

It was a very small room of a banality which rendered such precautions ridiculous or dramatically effective depending on temperament or mood. Atwater had long been a member. Entering, he couldn't imagine why or how he had been absent so long. It hadn't changed; rather it stood four-square in a shifting world. One wall was devoted to a some way sub-Bratby mural of Marx and Engels playing snakes-and-ladders; it had seemed rather *passé* even when painted by a South African called Schreiber to pay a bar-bill in 1954. Marx's left eye still showed the knife-wound made by Robert MacBryde. MacBryde had had some difficulty in explaining to Adolf, the milk-drinking queen whose club it was, that he had nothing against Marx, but had aimed the knife at a Scots poet whose accent suggested Mayfair.

'It's no ma faut the bugger moved,' he had said.

Such glories were in the past. Adolf was still there. Atwater was interested to observe that he had moved on from milk and was now more trendily spooning yoghourt into his absurdly small mouth.

He looked at Atwater, the spoon poised, yoghourt dripping.

'You owe me three-and-six,' he said. 'I forgot to mention it last time you were here. It's long overdue, I ought to charge interest really, God knows what it would come to, dearie, if I did. Still, it's nice to see you. Don't get so many nice boys here these days, can't complain though, not today I can't, got a lovely boy here today. Stevie, shift your lovely fanny, dear, and say hello to Atwater, one of my oldest friends he is.'

He beckoned to a young blond with prematurely decaying features who sat twitching on a bar-stool.

'Stuff it, you old nance,' said the blond.

'Isn't he coarse,' tittered Adolf, 'oooh isn't he coarse, how Ivor would have gone for him. I still miss Ivor, you know, dearie. Strange isn't it, some you do and some you don't. What can I do you for, dearie?'

'I'd like some gin,' said Atwater.

'Lovely gin here, made it this morning. Best quality, Mr Gordon would like the recipe.'

'Christ,' said the blond, 'I feel fucking awful.'

Atwater said, 'You don't look at all well. You're a most peculiar colour.'

'You see,' said Adolf. 'What did I tell you? Mr Atwater's a man of discrimination. He knows, dearie. You'd much better go to bed, I'll show you where.'

'Keep your fucking hands off me,' said the blond. He got to his feet and stumbled across the room, barging through the door marked 'Gents'.

'He's very rough, much too rough even for me, dearie,' Adolf said, smirking. ''Course he's nowhere to go, the rozzers are after him.'

'What for?'

'Well, we don't ask, do we, hardly polite now.'

Adolf took out a pink plastic comb lacking several teeth and with great care began to spread his lank black hair over his bald patch.

'Atwater.'

The other person in the room who had appeared to be dead or asleep with his head on the table in the corner where, such were the cleaning arrangements, he might conceivably have remained, ignored, for months, had come to life. He now sat up in the dark corner like Marius among the ruins of Carthage. An eye gleamed redly. He repeated in a wondering boom:

'Atwater.'

With resignation Atwater recognised Colonel Beazley.

'Of all men else I have avoided thee,' he remarked easily. 'Give the man some gin, Adolf.'

'You've seen my wife, Atwater . . .'

'Dearie me,' said Adolf.

The Colonel advanced with uncertain gait. Atwater inclined his head. Beazley put his hand on his shoulder and squeezed, painfully.

'And lived to tell the tale,' he said.

Atwater nodded again, modestly.

'You must tell me about it,' said the Colonel. 'When we are both stronger, that is. Meanwhile have you seen aught of Horridge?'

'No, I'm glad to say, no.'

'Won't have him in here,' said Adolf. 'He's not a nice man, Horridge.'

He removed a moody cap from a tub of hazelnut yoghourt.

'How well you put it,' Atwater said.

'Tried to bring a girl in here once. Sauce.'

'Really?'

'Black, too.'

'Atrocious.'

'American, I shouldn't wonder.'

'Can depravity go further?'

Colonel Beazley banged his fist on the bar.

'That'll do,' he said, and rubbed his hand for the blow had hurt. 'I'm worried about Horridge. He ought to flee the country. The police are on his track.'

'Can't blame them really. Not this time, dearie.'

'Any reason?'

'How should I know? My sources . . .' the Colonel, overcome, began to giggle.

'There sometimes is, but often of course,' reflected Atwater, considering his own position and resolving on optimism, 'not. The police frequently remind me of that Thurber cartoon.'

'Touché?'

'That, too, though it's not the one I was thinking of. It's the one where the Woman is saying to the Dog, "why don't you get out there and trace something?" It's often made me think of a police station. There they all are happily drinking cups of cocoa and the sergeant bangs in shouting "why don't you get out and trace something?"'

'Fanciful,' said the Colonel, 'very.'

Dr Ngunga was buttoning his boots. The girl in the bed said, 'You are awful . . .'

'Indeed.'

His tone was cold. He had divorced himself from what had gone before. It was mere carnality, satisfaction of his appetite, nothing to dwell on. Instead his mind roved in speculative realms; he contemplated the prospect of eternity.

'We are but as the dew,' he said.

'I've nothing against them myself, found some of them very generous I have, but you ought to hear my sister on the subject, goes on something awful she does.'

'The sun dissolves us.'

'What I said to her. Going to meet Horridge are you?'

'Horridge?'

Dr Ngunga's tone was blank even to the point of being ministerial.

'You want to watch him, he's a nasty bit of work. Did I ever tell you what he did to Vera, not to mention my cousin Violet? Perverted, that's what he is. Well we've all got our funny little ways, you have yourself, Doctor, no use denying it, but speaking for myself, I draw the line at chains, they're not nice. Then he's a nark.'

'I question that, indeed to goodness yes. Horridge is given to posing, he may preach anarchy, but he is, I fear, essentially a Social-Fascist. Some rough beast stumbling to Bethlehem, that catches him. But a nark, no. I tremble at the suggestion even while I reject it. Categorically.'

Heavy feet ascended the staircase and there was a banging at the door.

'This,' said the doctor alertly, 'is my cue. Mine not to reason why.'

He opened the window and stepped neatly out on to the tiles.

'Fend them off, my dear.'

The last she saw was a corner of dangling cape and then he was gone.

The knocking was re-doubled.

'When you saw my wife . . .'

'My heart bled for you, Colonel.'

'Indeed?'

'Copiously.'

'Tell you what,' said Adolf, 'maybe you'd better have a spot more gin, then I'm closing.'

'Closing?'

'This is monstrous.'

'Tell you what it is, ducks . . .'

'I should think so . . .'

'My boy-friend's a postman, got to be up at five, you know, so we close evenings now.'

'Don't believe a fucking word of it,' said the blond, emerging from the gents looking refreshed, ''e's past it, 'e's only an imaginary bugger now, even past wanking.'

'Why, you naughty boy, if that's what you think I'll . . .'

'What? Give me a demo, no thanks.'

'What about that gin then?' said Atwater, bored. This was a conversation he had too often endured.

'What gin was that?'

'The one we read about in the newspapers.'

'I don't know, I'm sure, hurt my feelings he has.'

'The fact is, Atwater, as I'm sure you realised, she's deranged, poor thing. This fixation on Horridge, you would think from listening to her, wouldn't you, that sex meant a lot to her?'

'She talked of the Duke of Windsor.'

'Postman, you couldn't stuff a letter-box.'

'Did she now? That's significant perhaps, though I'm sure she never . . .'

'A French fucking letter-box . . .'

'You mistake me, Colonel; she compared Horridge to the Duke.'

'Taller, surely.'

'He was a one.'

'Who?'

'The Duke, I remember once . . . ah dearie, long ago . . .'

Colonel Beazley shook his head so violently that his moustache (a rich mustard today) began to wobble. It was clear to Atwater that gloom was settling on him. The symptoms were by now familiar. Soon they might be afflicted by the sight of a strong man's tears.

'It's no good,' said the Colonel. 'She's mad again. Do you realise what it is to watch her faculties decay?'

'Why,' said Atwater, 'don't we go to see Polly?'

'Polly?'

'Your daughter.'

'Oh Polly, that Polly.'

'I've always fancied a uniform. You're too young, Stevie, to understand about that.'

'You're obscene, you great big lump of lard, do you know that, that's what you are, fucking obscene.'

'Oh yes.'

Atwater said, 'What about that gin?'

'I've always known that, Stevie, it's why I hide here. In this crazy cellar of a club, out of sight. Deep in the bowels of the city.'

At last the Colonel and Atwater mounted the stairs. Outside the fog had thickened. They stood watching for a taxi. The night was such that there seemed little chance of trying the Colonel's favourite tactics.

'Nevertheless,' said Atwater at the traffic lights.

'I'm fond of Adolf, you know.'

'Oh so am I.'

'An unfortunate manner, I grant you. But fundamentally a good egg. He was my batman. In the desert. Saved his life.

Or he saved mine. Something like that. One forgets the details. Drop in there once in a while, have a yarn. Now fades the glimmering landscape sort of mood. Not half fast enough I sometimes feel. Have you ever, Atwater, pray don't take offence, been in the bin?'

'No,' said Atwater, 'not that; not yet.'

He wished the Colonel would relax the grip on his arm.

'I'm afraid of it. My wife wants to put me away. A rest-cure, she calls it, but I'm cunning, I know better. Adolf's a very reassuring chap. Often set my mind at rest. Days gone by. When Monty wanted to court-martial me he just said, well we all know the General likes his little joke, and he was quite right. But he wasn't much help today. Difficult of course with that young brute there. You wouldn't think that was his son, would you?'

'No.'

'Fact I assure you.'

Mrs Hedge's call on Polly had been impulsive.

'I couldn't resist,' she had said, 'the opportunity of seeing you in your nest. I do hope my arrival hasn't ruffled your feathers.'

She gave a silvery tinkle and began to discuss the state of Polly's soul.

'I'm afraid,' said Polly, 'it's in a bad way.'

'We must see what we can do about that,' said Mrs Hedge, lifting the flap of her Pekingese's ear and whispering into it. Polly wriggled. It had been a mistake to sit on the divan.

'Would you like some coffee,' she said, 'or a drink?'

'It's a little early and coffee is bad for the soul.'

'Really?'

Mrs Hedge gave a little cough and cleared her throat. A silence ensued, pregnant with possibility.

'I wonder if you know what you mean to me . . .'

Polly shook her head.

'I am going to divulge to you what I have never divulged to a living soul . . . but need I say the words?'

'Oh no . . . I shouldn't.'

'Polly, may I . . .'

It was just then the doorbell rang and Polly leapt up to welcome Clare and Jeremy. The kiss she gave Clare had all the exuberance of relief. It smote Mrs Hedge with a shaft of jealousy, yet left her thinking,

'At least she can't be entirely . . .'

Even to herself the hateful word remained unframed.

Jeremy said, 'Well, my God, we've . . .'

Clare said, 'Darling, I must tell you, well I told you we were investigating, look it's too terribly exciting, is there anywhere we can talk, can we go into the kitchen, darling, super, well you'll never guess but guess, no, well then the country's gone quite mad, starkers, ravers, do you know what, we've had three visits from the police at the office, different ones too . . .'

'Clare, this is exciting, go on . . .'

'First, no that's wrong, first they came and said, did we know where Atwater could be found, so I said, goodness you don't mean my Atwater . . .'

'Yours, Clare?'

'Well sort of, I mean I found him and I had to say something, so I said of course I didn't but I rather fancied he was abroad. And they said, well, no, it couldn't be like that because they'd checked and he'd never had a passport, so I said, well what about Mr Stonehouse, and they went rather red, both of them, one was rather dishy by the way, I expect that's why they go in pairs, because they'd slipped up there of course.'

'That was very clever of you.'

'Wasn't it? So then, eventually they saw they weren't going to get anything out of me, that I was a clam, so they went away.'

'Poor Atwater, how boring for him.'

'Yes, indeed, then half an hour later another pair dropped in asking extraordinary questions about someone called Dr Ngunga. So I said, who the hell's Dr Ngunga?'

'A woolly lamb.'

'That's not what they said. They said he was a dangerous revolutionary. A psychopath, one of them said.'

'What nonsense.'

'Must say that particular fuzz looked pretty psychopathic himself. So then I said I'd never heard of him, such a relief to speak the truth, and they said they'd traced him to us through one of the Shropshire clients. Well then of course I couldn't say anything, because, well, you don't know, but the Shropshire clients they're like the MCC in our office or the Holy Ghunsest. You can't say a thing against them.'

'It sounds very stupid,' Polly said. 'He's a Fellow of All Souls. Failed.'

'That shows you. But finally, are you listening, what are you doing there?'

'I was just taking a peep to see how Jeremy and Rosemary are getting on.'

'Is it all right?'

'Oh it's fine. She's telling him about the trade gap.'

'Poor Jeremy, still I dare say it'll be good for him.'

'Well, he ought to know about the trade gap. Go on. This is exciting.'

'Well the third time, you'll never guess who they wanted the third time . . .'

'Groucho Marx?'

'No.'

'Weidenfeld or Nicolson?'

'No.'

'Well then I give up, I can't think of anyone more improbable, one of your Shropshire clients maybe?'

'No. Jeremy.'

'Jeremy.'

'Jeremy.'

'But why? Did they give a reason?'

Clare shook her head.

'Not, perhaps, boys?'

'Nuh-huh.'

'Choirboys or scouts, that sort of thing, I mean.'

'No I asked him at once, natch, but he says no.'

71

'Well he would, wouldn't he?'

'But he went pink.'

'He's always pink.'

'Yes, I know, but there's a certain shade when he's embarrassed but not telling a lie. It's very strange, isn't it?'

'Very,' Polly said. 'I think we should have a bottle of champagne. It's awfully good for thinking.'

'You are rich.'

'It fell off a lorry.'

'Really?'

'Well, Horridge brought it, so . . .'

Clare took a sip that turned into a swig.

'Oooh,' she said, 'it is good. There's always something about champagne. You know I wondered. Do you think there's been a coup and they're rounding up dissident elements?'

'Could be. Would you call Jeremy dissident?'

Clare sighed.

'Not really. But they're often against queers, aren't they?'

'Who?'

'People who go in for coups. And Atwater, he's dissident.'

'Atwater,' Polly said, looking at the bubbles in her glass, 'is rather wonderful, in an odd way.'

'Oh yes, he's so funny, he makes me laugh, but you could call him dissident, couldn't you?'

'Oh yes, indeed. Awfully. And Dr Ngunga?'

'Well, it sounds meany, but he's black, isn't he?'

'Awfully.'

'Well they might be against blacks. I mean they're often real beasts, coupers. Do you think we should tell Mrs Hedge?'

'Why on earth?' Polly opened her eyes wide.

'Well,' said Clare, 'she's a politician, isn't she. I suppose it would concern her.'

'Still . . .'

'You don't think we should?'

'It would worry her, it's not her sort of thing.'

'Well you know her better than I do, darling, but I'd have thought she might be interested.'

Polly shook her head.

'No, no,' she said, 'she's got no time for that sort of politics, coups and so on, she prefers the trade gap.'

Jeremy in the sitting-room felt he had been given more information about the British economy than he really wanted and was relieved to see the girls come back into the room. Also he was worried by the police visit. Attempts to reassure himself by pretending that they wanted him for a parking offence or speeding were made unconvincing by his certainty of innocence. The fact that he felt at least technically innocent in all other directions was less convincing because where morals were concerned guilt was less clearly quantifiable.

'Isn't it awful, Polly?' he said. 'It's like some ghastly nightmare epidemic. What do you suggest?'

He had come to look on Polly as a sister though he hadn't told her this. Actually he looked on Clare rather as a sister too, which made going to bed with her another occasion for obscure guilt, obscure because he could never remember the word incest.

Polly said, 'I suggest we should all have a lot more champagne.'

Horridge strode through the wastes of South London, brooding, his face dark lined with deep scars. Care sat uneasily on his cheek from which the roses of boyhood had long faded. Livid cruelty gleamed in his eye; yet a considerate observer (a trendy cleric for example) might there discern signs of remorse and passion; sorrow, for others' pain, the desolation of South London's socially underprivileged, those who cared nothing for him, were withered none the less. Comparisons between them and oaks or pines lightning-scathed might appear far-fetched. Horridge could justify them. As he walked his lips moved; in spite of all, tears (such as angels weep) could not be stemmed.

Horridge felt cracks appearing in the wall of his personality. Wilson had told him there was a general alert out.

'You better take cover man, bogeys after you.'

Useless to ask how he knew. He could only twitter. Anyway it stood to reason: one as promiscuous as Wilson must pick up information as a sparrow crumbs.

Then he'd heard news of the raid. His whole stock of dynamite (Horridge was fundamentally old-fashioned) gone.

Anxious, he had begun to telephone; first, Harriet, his wife.

The voice that replied was unknown, refused to identify itself; a faint moaning could be heard in the background.

Conclusion: Special Branch had moved in there.

A call to Gertrude in her Norfolk fastness had gone unanswered; he fancied he could hear the howl of a Great Dane respond to the repetition of the bell.

Then in Pimlico he had seen Richie hustled to a police car, a blanket over his head, but his bushwackers' boots unmistakable.

Horridge had the uneasy feeling that the rules of the game had been changed. People were taking him more seriously than he had ever demanded. What had been the free expression of his personality was being enchained by the participation of others. He brooded. Yet even then felt the quickening of indomitable spirit. This infernal pit, he remarked to himself, could never hold him in bondage. He could not think submission, a word absent from his vocabulary. He resolved on war, open or understood.

The question was how. Mere anarchy was not enough. He made his way, brow furrowed, to the cellar where he had engaged to meet Wilson. Could he be trusted?

Colonel Beazley was silent in the taxi. Atwater found this the most alarming of the day's alarming events; to date. It was as if he was sitting beside an exhausted volcano. Atwater himself felt low. He would have liked to attribute this to the time of year. There was something depressing about the month. Introspectively he was aware of unsettling movement. In certain areas things were falling apart. They might re-assemble. It was sure to be less comfortable. The fact was, only the present could be lived in. Extraordinary thought.

'One's current way of life,' he said, 'is always the only possible.'

The Colonel sighed.

Atwater all but nudged him; it would soon be spring; lilac-blossom, good God, even hyacinths in gardens, and girls, he supposed.

He was pleased to find a party in progress at Polly's; just what they both needed.

Polly put her arms round him and kissed him on the mouth. Clare put her arms round him but his lips slid aside. Mrs Hedge regarded him with ice in her eye. It put Atwater on his mettle.

'Your face,' he said, 'is unfamiliar to me, but I feel sure I know your name.'

'This is Mrs Hedge.'

'The politician,' Clare said.

'Stateswoman, surely.'

'She's been telling me all about the Trade Gap,' Jeremy said.

'We must talk to you,' Clare said, 'me and Polly.'

Colonel Beazley woofed.

'Daddy,' Polly said, 'are you all right?'

He was holding a moustache in either hand, and, left-handed, blond handlebar one dangling, was tugging at that fixed in position.

'I'm afraid he's in a bad way,' Atwater said. 'He's been strangely silent in the taxi.'

'I must say,' said Mrs Hedge with the weighty authority of practice, 'he was behaving most oddly last night. Indeed I've been considering whether it might not be my duty to apprise my association of his condition. At the same time one must take into account all possible variables.'

'Are you a doctor?' asked Atwater.

'I would not presume.'

'I have some medical training myself,' Atwater said. 'I studied under Jungfleisch.'

'I confess . . .'

'No need, I am aware Jungfleisch is not orthodox. There lies his relevancy. You couldn't say the Colonel was orthodox, could you?'

'Indeed no, but I feel he should be made . . .'

'Made? Is this Tory freedom at work?'

'That allegation is . . .'

'Polly,' Atwater said, 'give me some gin. Not champagne, a liquor for youth, but gin, the old reliable. Mrs Hedge, Jungfleisch says that only experience can effect what he is still old-fashioned enough to term a cure, even though he is willing to admit that in a parasyllabic world, cure is a non-runner, since you will be ready to confess that we cannot inventory normality.'

'Harmonious action,' Colonel Beazley said.

'There you are,' said Atwater, 'thank you for the gin, my dear, how can you suggest the need of psychiatric treatment for one capable of such a synthesis of experience?'

'I'm afraid I don't know your name,' Mrs Hedge said, 'and I confess I have some difficulty in following your train of thought, but I feel obligated to tell you that psychiatric treatment for offenders, I mean the Colonel, has never crossed my mind. There are other methods. That, indeed, I regard as no better than exploded and discredited Liberalism. What I said however was that I considered it my duty to inform our association of his condition. It may mean nothing to you, but some of us have votes to lose.'

She pressed the Pekingese, apparently reluctant surrogate for Polly, to a fervent breast. It yelped.

'Something terrible has happened to your mother,' Colonel Beazley said. He put his arm round Polly and struck his heart. 'I feel it here.'

Mrs Hedge found the situation intolerable. Nevertheless she remained. The Lobby had long ago decided that tenacity was her great quality.

Polly disengaged herself from her father just in time to prevent him getting her head securely in Chancery. She approached Atwater and touched him on the cheek.

'Goodness gracious,' said Clare.

'Madam,' said the Colonel, 'we all have troughs, but,' he squared his shoulders, 'Beazley's himself again. What news on the Rialto?'

'Atwater . . .'

'Yes, my . . .'

'Have you heard you're in danger . . . the police . . . ?'

'Faugh, or rather, pshaw.'

'Do you mean that?'

'I assure you, Colonel, action is . . .'

'I don't give a fig for the police.'

Aloysius was going to end the night in clink. It was the penalty for striking a policeman. He couldn't explain why he had done so. It had seemed a good idea in the pub. Now it seemed less inspired. It would delay his search for Atwater. Fortunately the sergeant was an old friend.

'We'll see what we can do. Dare say someone clobbered you first, eh?'

'That's right, man,' said Aloysius, 'I just struck out blindly.'

'Don't we all,' sighed the policeman who was a philosopher. 'Don't worry, mate, there's a bugger two cells along we can pin it on.'

Dr Ngunga tiptoed over the roofs of London, nimble as a chamois.

'One more river and that's the river of Jordan,' he sang to himself.

Not for nothing had he once been an elder of the kirk in Dundee.

The mechanics of his getaway actually bored him. There had been too many. He had boarded small boats in remote estuaries, aeroplanes on disused runways in Lincolnshire and slipped out, disguised as a monsignor, in the Papal train. He had even been transported to Switzerland as a corpse. His resource, he knew well, was infinite.

'You remember you asked me a question?' Polly said.
'I did? Most unusual.'
'Yes, it was, for you.'
'Oh yes.'
'Well, I've decided . . .'
'Yes.'
'I'm not sleeping with Horridge any more . . . So . . .'
'Really?'
'Yes, I'll tell you, it just came to me, why should I? Horridge in his filthy way is good in bed but that's not everything . . .'
'It is when you're in bed surely?'
'Well, maybe but . . . don't you want to now?'
'Oh yes.'
'It wasn't what they call a passing whim, was it?'
'Oh no, indeed no, it doesn't seem like passing. Not just now.'
'So tonight.'
'Here?'
'Well, I don't expect they'd let me in to the Turkish Baths.'

Horridge could hear Wilson moan as he descended the steps of the ruined bomb shelter.
'Why you want to meet me here, man?'
'I ought to beat you to pulp.'
'Please God no, baby. That what you fancy, baby, I gotta friend would be happy to oblige. Happy I assure you.'
'Wilson,' Horridge said, 'was it you that split?'
Wilson rolled his eyes in an old-fashioned mannerism he'd admired in the cinema.

Horridge would have liked to sit down. Pride kept him standing.

'Why'd you bring me here, Horridge baby?'

'For your own safety.'

'My safety, precious baby, you don' need to worry 'bout my safety.'

'Why not?'

'Some of my best frien's is fuzz.'

Horridge drew back his fist and checked, appalled. He paled. He had been in imminent danger of practising what he had so often preached. If he'd been a Catholic he would have crossed himself. As it was he took a pill. The game was over.

The fog settled over London. From the river came the melancholy sound of horns. Adolf, waking in bed with Stevie straddled over him, was alarmed to see it rub its back on the window-pane. Harriet Horridge, moaning as she had for weeks in her dressing-gown, began feverishly to turn the knobs of her radio in a vain attempt to discover whether it was night or day. Dr Ngunga crouched against a chimney-stack. He remembered that Macaulay, crossing the Irish Sea on a steamer, had sat all night on deck going through *Paradise Lost* in his head and had never enjoyed it more; Dr Ngunga found half-way through the third book that he couldn't agree and switched to Dante. Colonel Beazley sat in an armchair, his hand clutching Mrs Hedge's. 'This'll compromise you,' he said. The thought revived him and he began to chortle. 'There's no news like the *News of the World*,' he crooned. Jeremy snored in an armchair while Clare, curled in another, dreamed that one after another the Shropshire clients, actually gentlemen in England now a-bed, raped her ceremonially in the paddock at Ascot while the Silver Ring shouted the odds; occasionally she gave a cat-like moan of pleasure. In the Turkish Baths an attendant raised the alarm and search was made for Atwater while he, in fact in bed with Polly, made unpractised and at first apologetic love. However, she

79

soon found a position that suited. Later she fell asleep in his arms and in her dreams her Exmoor pony was restored to her. But Atwater, a rare feeling in his loins, lay awake all night, pondering. As when a mighty river that has meandered without apparent aim through dead plains and stagnant tropical forest of a sudden emerges into rocks and tumbles over cataracts changing its character utterly or when a lion long caged in a dark and foetid den regains its liberty, blinks in the unaccustomed sunlight, stretches its limbs warily before pricking its way across the vast and silent empty plains of Africa, so he; or so it seemed.

Rum.

Meanwhile night crept on. The day approached.

In an office, many fathoms down, a figure of great depth and cryptic importance leafed through files. He said, 'Look here, why are we pursuing people who haven't stamped insurance cards?'

'Glad you asked that, sir. Routine inquiry, we're calling it.'

'But dammit, we're counter-espionage.'

'Yes, sir, that's right. Got it in one, you have, sir.'

'Well, then, I may be very stupid.'

'Wouldn't say that, sir.'

'You wouldn't? Good.'

'Not my place, sir.'

'I should think not. Well, then . . .'

'Well, sir, it's like this, sir. 'Course we're counter-espionage, but we can't let on that's what we are, can we now, sir? Stands to reason. Official Secrets Act. I mean to say, sir, you won't take offence, now will you, sir, but there was quite a discussion, I think I'm at liberty to reveal, about whether you should be informed of our role.'

'But dammit, I'm head of the department.'

'Exactly, sir, that shows how secret it is. So, sir, that being so, naturally we've got to keep quiet about what we actually exist to do and the consequence is, we find ourselves getting landed with this sort of work. It's a front, you might say if you know the expression, sir. And there are other advantages too, apart of course from correlation, always vital in the CS correlation, you'll agree. First, sir, I'd like to point out that it's extremely rare to find an enemy agent who's stamping his insurance card. Now, sir, you'll be aware of course how the Americans . . .'

'Americans . . .'

'I know it's painful, sir, I'm aware you were based in Washington. Still they strike it lucky from time to time. You'll remember perhaps, sir, how they came to arrest that gangster fellow, Capone. Hadn't paid his income tax, had he, silly chap. Well, sir, brooding on that gave the great man, yes, sir, it came direct from him, in his bath he was actually, when he had this idea, took his pipe from his mouth and said, "if we clobber everyone who hasn't paid his tax or stamped his insurance card, it's statistically probable"— nuts on statistics, he is, sir—"that we'll rope in every foreign agent in the country." Well, sir, this came through to us, it was on tape of course, we tape everything he says, every single word he utters, just for the historical significance, you'll understand, and this seemed just the ticket. So there we are, sir. I'm very bucked by it personally.'

'But there must be millions.'

'That's right, sir. Biggest security sweep in history.'

III

'It's funny, isn't it, a few weeks ago we were all wanted by the fuzz and now here we all are and nobody's bothering us. Not that I'm complaining of it, merely observing it's rum.'

Jeremy was, it occurred to Atwater, a little less pink, more inclined to terracotta, these days. On the other hand he was fatter. He looked more confident behind his desk too.

'Well, be that as it may, what can I do for you, Atwater?'

Atwater didn't like the tone; unctuous. Clearly being wanted by the police hadn't done Jeremy any good.

'The condition of my grandmother's estate . . .'

'The wheels are in motion.'

'Can't they be quickened?'

'Impossible.'

'You alarm me.'

A prolonged and unseasonable frost had caused the cancellation of all race meetings for some time past. Atwater didn't trust the dogs despite the eager promptings of Aloysius.

'No,' he had said, 'they simply aren't me. There would be a distressing lack of harmony.'

Accordingly he found himself a bit short and had come to Jeremy.

Jeremy began to tap the ends of his fingers together. He looked more and more like an Ealing actor playing a Dickensian lawyer. Atwater was flummoxed.

He said, 'It was a curious incident, the police scare. Myself, I think it ultimately political. Mrs Hedge claims it was a plot to discredit her. That seems to me fanciful. Rather it was the coming to the surface of archetypal fears, yet conceivably manipulated by government agencies. *Divide et impera*, you know. There is no word of Horridge yet?'

'Abso-bally-lutely vanished. Bizarre, yes?'

'Very.'

82

Horridge had been seen by none since the night of the scare. It was as if he had been spirited away.

'It's true,' Atwater said, 'the world is a quieter, even perhaps a cleaner and better, place without him, but I confess I miss the fool. It's had repercussions too, his disappearance. Lady Gertrude's attempted suicide, to mention only one.'

'I heard about that.'

'It worried Polly.'

'Must have.'

Not only did Jeremy seem less pink and more confident; Atwater also sensed a massive lack of interest; there was none of that gauche willingness to please that had been such an agreeable part of his character.

'You must excuse me, Atwater,' he said now, 'but I have another client.' He pressed a buzzer and smiled seraphically. 'From Shropshire,' he said.

Atwater to his astonishment found himself being ushered out. A tweed suit containing a body brushed past him.

In the outer office, Clare said, 'Atwater darling, could you be an angel and wait two minutes and then take me out to lunch?'

Her eyes were red-rimmed, but this did not prevent Atwater, chivalrous, from assenting.

'There's a Greek restaurant.'

'Greek?'

'There are days I feel very Greek. Darling Atwater, it is nice to see you. Tell me, are you going to marry Polly?'

'Marry Polly?'

'That's right.'

'It's an idea.'

'Don't be provoking.'

'I can't talk about marriage before lunch. It's not done on an empty stomach.'

Atwater was pleased to discover that the food wasn't very Greek; about as Aegean as Notting Hill was how he put it.

'I'm glad of that,' he said, 'my sentiments are more Greek than my belly.'

'Do you remember?'

'Everything and nothing. What's wrong with Jeremy?'

'Oh, Atwater, it's terrible, I'm so glad you asked, do you know I don't know. It happened just like that. I think his uncle's been talking to him, nasty old man, well I know he has because he gave him the affairs of one or two of the Shropshire clients (the younger ones of course) to handle and this is the result . . .'

'He's reverted to type.'

'No, not that, no, you can't mean . . .'

'I'm afraid so, he's become an English Gentleman.'

He couldn't blame Clare for beginning to cry again.

'I wondered,' she said, 'when Benny got his cards.'

'Who was Benny?'

'The lift-boy.'

'Ah, I should have guessed . . . with a name like that what else could he be?'

Atwater walked through the darkening streets. Freezing again. No racing tomorrow. He blew on his nails, an old-fashioned practice he had never known to be effective. He went into a call-box and dialled Polly's number.

'It's me.'

'Why's your voice like that?'

'I'm speaking through a handkerchief.'

'Why?'

'The smell in this box. Acrid and ammoniac and quite repellent. Shall I come round?'

'Yes . . . what is it?'

There was alarm in her rising voice. She had had a premonition of disaster. She was always having them now. Her mother's attempt to gas herself (thwarted only by a wildcat strike) and her father's rapid and seemingly uncheckable decline (he had taken to declaiming the works of Sir Henry Newbolt, with emphasis on Clifton Chapel, at Speakers' Corner on Sundays) were teaching her to anticipate the worst; it was clear that the Exmoor pony could not be held to represent the extreme of woe. So now when she heard first a knocking, then a splutter and was then cut off, she prepared for just that, the worst. Yet being a tough and realistic girl she checked herself. It was unlikely after all that Horridge had returned. Something told her that he was on a long journey to some undiscovered country.

She sat in the dark and waited.

Atwater would come.

Atwater, however, was in difficulties. Hearing the knock he had looked up and been profoundly bored to see a policeman. He had the feeling he'd sat round the movie.

The policeman beckoned.

'Makes more work for us, that does.'

'What?' said Atwater.

'Saucy, are you? Pretend you don't know?'

'No pretence, I assure . . .'

'It's an indictable offence, that's what.'

Atwater started to raise an eyebrow, checked himself.

'I'd take you in, I would, down to the station. I'd enjoy working you over, personalised like. I'm good at it, you know . . .'

Atwater wondered if it would be wise to say he was sure of it and decided the safest role was merely nodder.

'If it wasn't for the missus, that's what I'd do. But it takes time you know, a proper working over and she'd never forgive me if we was late for the ballet. Crazy on the ballet, she is, well, I like it myself, ever so tasteful the ballet, bleeding poofs of course but it takes all sorts and at least they're not bleeding niggers, just as God made 'em I suppose, but, Mister, I warn you . . .' He dug his fingers deep into Atwater's shoulder. 'Just let me catch you at these larks again and it's pulp you'll be. I'll enjoy it too. I don't have the advantage of that Public School balls, none of this "it hurts me more than it hurts you". My way, it fucking well hurts you and it's fun for me. Now hop it.'

'Quite,' said Atwater.

He began to think of retiring to the suburbs.
Where men are gardeners.

'You ever been in the nick, Adolf?' said Richie.
'Wouldn't really like to say.'
''Course he 'as,' Stevie said, 'time and again, the old cock-sucker.'
'D'you know . . .' Richie's voice was plaintive; one more travelled than Adolf might have been reminded of a hungry dingo wailing in the outback. 'It was five hours before I twigged they thought I was Horridge.'
'You ought to sue them for that. Character defamation, that is.'
'Yeah, I ought, oughtn't I?'

'I'm afraid,' Atwater said, 'the police have taken to acting autonomously.'
'Oh no.'
'No other explanation fits. There I was, in the telephone-box, shielding myself from germs which can't be called anti-social . . .'
'Yes, you told me.'
They were in bed together. It was, Polly felt, a good time of day to be in bed, late afternoon. She liked drinking gin and tonic after whoring around so it was only sensible to go to bed when other people were having tea. She'd worked this out all by herself. She felt for the moment happy; pleasantly, warmly, stickily, damply happy. Atwater was getting much better at it too.
'Perhaps,' she said, 'he thought you were giving a bomb warning.'
'Absurd.'
'They speak through handkerchiefs to disguise their voices.'
'Who do?'
'Bomb warners.'

'Very silly. If I ever planted a bomb I wouldn't go about warning people. It would be because I wanted to blow them up.'

'Everybody isn't logical like you, darling . . . Darling?'

Atwater was wary; he mistrusted the tone.

'My glass is empty.'

He fished beside the bed.

'Here's the bottle.'

'But the ice is in the fridge.'

'Let it stay there.'

'Please.'

'It bruises the gin.'

'I like my gin bruised.'

'Oh all right then . . .'

He padded on bare feet, naked, to the kitchen, aware that this surrender to Polly's will was the price paid for something he identified with hesitation as necessary, even enjoyable. It belonged to the movement in his life. He had moments of distrust, moments of fear, was at once for and against; yet accepted it as the rhythm he was moving to.

He bent over the sink, extracting ice-cubes with familiar difficulty. There was a knock at the window. Atwater looked up.

'Polly, there's a face at the window.'

'Goodness.'

'I'm going to let it in.'

He pulled the cord that raised the skylight window. The face disappeared and a leg was thrust through the widening aperture. Another followed, then, predictably, a torso. So far, so good. With a leap the figure was at Atwater's feet. He bent down and offered a courteous and helping hand. He raised a middle-aged man of quite unusual anonymity of feature.

'Where is she?'

'Who?'

'My wife?'

'Well?' called Polly from the bed.

'It's a lunatic.'

'How do you know?'

87

'He's looking for his wife.'

'Goodness, how sad.'

'I assure you,' said Atwater, 'you are deceived. Barking as you might say through the wrong skylight. There are no wives here, not even for ready money.'

'Don't believe you . . .'

'Have some gin then, guaranteed to aid credulity.'

Polly came through to the kitchen. Unlike Atwater she had wrapped a dressing-gown round her. As usual, she looked more than usually fetching. It was a philosophical problem he might get round to working on some day, when he was in the mood for philosophy, how she continually contrived to look more than usually fetching. If that was how she usually looked—and it was—how then did she look usually? It was, he felt, the sort of question that might have kept Descartes hard at work in his stove for a winter or two. On the other hand a very similar sort of problem had finished Bertrand Russell for philosophy and turned him on to politics, sex and sociology, which suggested that he, Atwater, should go carefully on this one.

Polly now spoke. 'Darling,' she said.

'I'm sorry, I was just getting the ice when this gentleman dropped in.'

'What would I do without you, thanks. You'll catch cold.'

'I don't think so. Decent of you to . . .'

'Why, Mr Hedge, I didn't recognise you for a moment. Atwater, it's Mr Hedge.'

'Where is she?' said Mr Hedge, dogged.

'He's looking for his wife,' Atwater said. It seemed odd when one thought of Mrs Hedge which was of course as rarely as possible. Not only was she in his opinion a bitch, she was also undeniably a politician. Say what you could for her, that couldn't be wiped out. Atwater was of Sir Toby's opinion; he had liefer be a Brownist than a politician.

'Where is she?'

'But, Mr Hedge, I'm her problems secretary, not her appointments one.'

'I found her diary.'

'Any good?'

Mr Hedge shivered. Atwater was intrigued. A diary that could induce a shivering fit in one so obstinately English and minor Public School as Mr Hedge was surely a document worth reading.

'I wouldn't have believed it,' said Mr Hedge. (Atwater was convinced his teeth were clenched.)

'What?'

'What she said.'

'Go on.'

'Always thought you a nice girl, fancied you even, tell the truth.'

Polly sat down.

'I think there's something wrong,' she said.

'Uh-huh.'

'This diary,' Atwater said, 'have you got it with you?'

Mr Hedge went back into his shivering routine. Atwater found himself thinking better of Mrs Hedge. Whatever her failings in other respects she was clearly no slouch when it came to diaries. It sounded the sort of thing the Marquis de Sade or Jack the Ripper might have kept if they'd been a bit more diligent, aware of their duty to posterity, etc.

'I think,' Mr Hedge said, 'I'm going to be sick . . . it's called Lesbianism I'm told.'

'Really,' Atwater said as he took his arm, 'the bathroom's through here.'

A moment later they were saddened by the sound of a strong man vomiting.

'Atwater,' Polly said, 'why don't you put some clothes on. Mr Hedge will be embarrassed when he realises you are naked.'

'You may be right.' Atwater fetched shirt and trousers. 'I should like to see this diary.'

'Do you think it's really about me?'

'Well, it must be, mustn't it, to bring that loony here.'

'It's not true, you know, Mrs Hedge and me.'

'Well, I didn't think it was. I mean, it's more likely she's mad and imagining things than you're mad and doing them.'

89

'Mad?'

'With Mrs Hedge?'

'Sorry about that,' said Mr Hedge, coming out of the bathroom with a glass of water in his hand. 'Turned my stomach, that's what thinking about it did.'

'Mr Hedge,' Atwater said, 'perhaps we should see this diary. If I understand you right, your wife claims in this diary that a Lesbian relationship exists between her and Polly here. Is that the case?'

'Disgusting, that's what . . .'

'Well,' Atwater spoke with some approach to warmth. 'You can take it from me it's all balls.'

Polly began to giggle.

'It's very clear,' said Mr Hedge. 'Explicit.'

Polly said, 'I'll tell you what I think, Mr Hedge. I think you don't want to worry about it. I think it's just what we call in politics a policy statement. We're always drawing them up, Mrs Hedge and me, all part of our work to save the country.'

'Don't see this sort of stuff saving the country. Mucky, that's what it is, mucky.'

'No, no, Mr Hedge, she's done this one on her own, but, listen, the point is, these policy statements, nobody in politics ever expects to do anything about them. They're just a way of relieving their feelings.'

'Like masturbating,' said Atwater.

'Not nowadays,' said Mr Hedge. 'When I was a boy, a bit different, disgusting too, that is though, if you don't grow out of it.'

'You mistake me,' Atwater said, 'I was making a comparison, not asking a question.'

'And now she's . . . she's vanished,' said Mr Hedge.

'Well, that's something,' said Atwater.

'I don't know about that. Might have thought so once, you know, I'm not a fool . . . but I can't help thinking it's unfair. Things ought to stay as they were.'

Atwater sensed a great deep sadness in Mr Hedge. He felt

for him; his gums bled in sympathy. Mutability had never been to his taste either.

'There was none of this when I married Rosemary,' said Mr Hedge.

'You can't be sure there is now,' Polly said.

'It's there in her diary. You can't argue with diaries. Anyway I was thinking about politics. The Young Conservatives now, YC's we used to call ourselves, that was something different . . . I was one myself, not for the politics, mind you, but for the dancing and the tennis. I met Rosemary there; she was called Rosie then.'

Atwater saw it all; the marquee at the Surrey club, the mixed doubles final, then the evening dancing to Joe Loss's third band, Rosie in her pale blue, almost daringly off-the-shoulder, gown that later brushed the dew as they made their arm-linked way to the Morris Cowley in the car park. The declaration under the laburnum trees of Woking, the squeezed hand, the inexperienced kiss, then home to the parental 'Cedars', good-night on the doorstep under the Home Counties moon. He'd read about it somewhere.

'Now,' said Mr Hedge, 'she wants to be Chancellor of the Exchequer. They make a joke of it in the office.'

'Poor, poor Mr Hedge,' said Polly.

'Where's Mr Atwater, Jerry?'

'Haven't seen him in a while back, sir, not been in, sure he hasn't now.'

Richie sighed. 'Want a word with him. Got his head screwed on, Atwater has. I'm in a bit of what he'd call a dilemma.'

'Heard you'd got married again.'

'Yeah . . . well . . . that's just it.'

'Congratulations.'

'What d'you mean . . . congratulations? This some of that goddam Irish blarney? You congratulate a man when he falls neck-deep in shit?' Richie took a brooding pull on his frosty, assessing the damage, like Prometheus after the vulture had moved on. 'It's a bad habit with me, marriage. I got it the way some folks have mice and others leprosy.'

'No good asking Atwater then, baby.' Aloysius had entered the bar, an orchid in his button-hole; he was mysteriously aware, with an intuition that might have disturbed one more sensitive or observant than Richie, of what they had been saying. 'I gotta news. Atwater's on the slippery path himself. Last time I saw him, man, he had devotion in his face.'

'Devotion . . . Holy cow.'

'Yeah, man, an' the love-light shone there like the lights on Broadway.'

'You been on Broadway, Aloysius baby?' inquired an ever-sceptical Wilson.

'Sure I been on Broadway. I been just 'bout every place you can name. Fact, mo' places, mos' probably, than you can name. Whadya doin' anyways joinin' men here, you catamite you, Wilson? Don' you know this is a bar for real men, ain't that so, Mas' Richie?'

'You said it,' growled Richie, eyeing the elegant Wilson with disgust that extended, ever deepening, to take in the nameless Jewish novelist he saw lurking on the circumference of the group.

'Sure I know that, Aloysius baby. Why you think I'm here, man?'

'Wilson, you is plain incorrigible. One of these bright days you gonna walk into trouble, plenty trouble.'

'My, my.'

'Atwater,' Aloysius said, 'ain't what he was or what he promised to be. One o' what the poet Wordsworth called dem glorious-mornin' boys. I sure is disappointed. You know my proposition of employment to him, Richie man, well he jus' wouldn't listen. Said it wasn't feasible. Deaf to reason, the man was, like a tom-cat in a rut. 'Tain't natural.'

'Doesn't sound like Atwater.'

Richie dropped his eyes. He sought elucidation in his beer. Or at least support. He looked like an augur; despairing but stoic also. His contemplation was disturbed by two bony fingers being thrust into his midriff, causing him to jerk the beer.

'Thus spake Zarathustra . . . he is working my purpose out.'

The accompanying snigger rather than the words helped Richie identify the novelist. He clenched and drew back a huge Antipodean fist . . .

'Thought I told you to keep out of my ruddy way or you get smashed, see. Poking your fucking nose in where it's not wanted.'

'My, my . . . *comme c'est* butch . . .'

'Don't be naïve, you Aussie burk, how else can I get my novel written?'

Aloysius, a literary critic, considered the objection.

'Man's got a point there, Richie,' he said, 'how else can he?'

'Who the fuck wants him to?'

'Why,' Wilson cried, 'there's Stevie. Baby. Over here, baby, quick, I do believe there's goin' to be a fight . . . why, give me creepy-crawlies, Jeremy lovey, you too, I ain't seen you Jeremy dahlin' in a month o' blue movies. You ditched yo' Shropshire clients, Jerry boy?'

'All I ask,' Richie stuck to his theme with the pertinacity required by the first settlers in Botany Bay (if they wished to make good), 'is, out of my fucking way.'

'You overdo it.'

'What?'

'Fucking.'

'Alimony I pay I guess I got a right to.'

'Why, Jerry baby, sure I know 'bout yo' Shropshire clients. Some o' my best friends is Shropshire. Stevie boy here's my all-time favourite Shropshire lad though, ain't you, Stevie baby?'

'It's funny, Atwater darling, we do all our drinking at home now. Don't you miss them?'

Atwater shook his head. He was sitting in an armchair,

93

Polly on the floor in front of him, her head against his knees. It didn't worry him that she couldn't see him shake his head.

'The pubs, I mean.'

'Oh pubs.'

'We'll go back I expect, some time. I had lunch with Clare today. She says she haunts them. She isn't happy.'

'Poor Clare.'

'We'll be buying television next, that's what it'll come to.'

'Ah, maybe we should.'

'Atwater.'

'For Mr Hedge, I mean.'

He glanced across the room where Mr Hedge was sitting like one of the more unsuccessful exhibits in the Natural History Museum.

'He keeps asking me to call him Mervyn. I don't like to somehow.'

'It's not much of a name.'

'Not much of a name, it's an awful name. It's almost all he does say though.'

'That's why I thought, perhaps television, take him out of himself.'

'Take himself out of here'd be better. How long's he been here?'

'Weeks and weeks.'

The mouth on the face opposite opened.

'Rosie's changed, that's what it is. Don't know why she couldn't stay as she was. We were all right as we were.'

It had been some time before Mrs Hedge noticed that her husband was missing; she had her work to do. Indeed but for the promptings of her flesh, its quickening surges, when she thought of Polly, particularly how her hair rested on her nape, she would have had no private life at all. It was swallowed up in duty. She had remarked on this in the Commons, on the radio, television and public platforms, dwelling on the contrast between her selfless devotion to the Common Weal and the greedy pursuit of personal advantage characteristic of certain interest groups located for the most part, she was sorry to have to say, in Northern and Midland conurbations.

It was by speaking like this that she had made her reputation.

Even when she realised that she hadn't seen Mr Hedge for some time, she merely assumed that he was off on a selling trip. She accepted this. Generously she didn't grudge him his work. 'Every man must labour in the vineyard,' she had been known to say, 'without the debasing and delusory support of social security,' she had wittily added, thus bringing the house, as it were, down.

Nor did Polly tell her where she could find her husband even when she remarked that this was surely a selfishly prolonged selling trip, almost a jaunt. Polly felt that Mr Hedge needed a rest, time to sort his problems out. She took his problems more seriously than she took his wife's. But she was sorry for her too. It was a pity she didn't feel like obliging her.

'The thing is,' she told Clare, 'I don't think it would really make her happier.'

'Don't you?'

'No. What she wants is to be Chancellor. It would just get in her way.'

'Well you know her better than I do.'

'That's true. You see, more and more, I feel it's all a matter of finding a balance.'

'Finding a balance?'

'Yes, otherwise your life's just confusion. Like poor Daddy's. Now Mrs Hedge has found hers, you see.'

'I think I follow and I'm sure you're right. It's like Jeremy. He was much happier while he was just concentrating on the Shropshire clients.'

'Isn't he still?'

'Alas no, he's set up a menage.'

'Really?'

'*A trois.*'

'Heavens.'

Atwater lay in bed alone. Polly was at work, saving the country. Atwater didn't mind. It paid the rent. His inspiration in the betting-shops hadn't returned. He felt, sometimes but not too often, like the poet Wordsworth. He had been told he could draw no more in anticipation of his grandmother's estate. He would soon be back financially where he had been too often before. The matter required thought. He preferred to have nothing to do with it. Thought wasn't the thing. It led to care. He was sure, again with Sir Toby, that care was an enemy of life. Besides thought as such, as an intellectual exercise or rather except as an intellectual exercise, was worthless. It was all in the Bible, adding cubits to your stature. Let intuition or instinct, as he had remarked in many a saloon and public bar, guide all. It was their reliance on instinct that accounted for the superior practicality of women. That was the real joke on Mrs Hedge. Entering the man's world of conscious manipulation of the intellect she'd opted for an inferior and far less satisfying expression of her practicality. After all, nobody since the Greeks at least had seen any real efficacy in philosophy. And that was the pure roving intellect. Therefore . . .

Atwater could go on like this for hours, especially in bed.

Meanwhile, on the sofa, Mr Hedge lay in a drugged slumber, dreaming of tennis dresses and damp laurels.

'Clarici . . .'
'I thought we weren't speaking.'
'But I'm in trouble.'
'Jeremy, haven't you learned yet, you're always in trouble.'
'Please, I don't know what my uncle . . .'
'Frig your uncle.'
'Clarici, can I come now and see you?'
'Can't you tell me on the telephone?'
'Imposs . . . please.'
'Oh all right.'
She put down the receiver.

'You'll have to go, I'm afraid. It would embarrass him terribly to find you here.'

'Young puppy.'

'I almost love you when you say young puppy.'

'Young puppy, young puppy, young puppy.'

'Yum, yum.'

'Now frig me again, wish I enjoyed it any other way.'

Colonel Beazley sat watching the grey waves of England with morose attention. Newbolt hadn't worked. He had left London and come to Brighton, found a jolly little pub and hated it. They sang in the evening. Intolerable. Sometimes they were songs of Sussex. Monstrous. Meanwhile he still felt oppressed. He telephoned his wife once a day. They had let her home on condition she abstained from sculpture. The psychiatrist asserted this was at the root of her troubles. Bloody fool, as the Colonel, who knew a thing or two about troubles, could have told him. Anything you did was merely an expression of your troubles. If people were perfectly happy they would feel no need for action. So he'd taken a step in the right direction. He'd decided to stop speaking to people. But he couldn't stop telephoning. Worse, words kept forming in his head. Somehow, he'd got to get beyond them. Stop thinking in words, Beazley, think in images, he said to himself.

Below him the sea surged throwing up grey flecks as it struck the wall. The Boy and his girl leaned on the rail contemplating eternity, sin and absolution. They were eating potato crisps from an old-fashioned bag with the salt in blue paper. They had a can of Coca-Cola between them. It stood on the ground at their feet, upright as a denial. An old man passed, head bowed; he was returning from work. A samphire gatherer, one of the last in England. A dreadful trade. The Boy was speaking to the girl. She understood what he was saying. It didn't diminish his sense of aloneness. In fact, it intensified it. A large-breasted woman in a fur wrap passed them. She was singing,

> 'How you gonna keep 'em down on the farm
> After they've seen Paree . . .?'

Colonel Beazley nodded his head. He saw it all, took it in, understood. He began to cry. His upper lip was bare.

Harriet Horridge descended the stairs of her Fulham tenement. She wore a dressing-gown of dead grey wool. Her mouth was slack, her eyes glaucous. She stood at the door of the flats. When a man approached she pulled the top of the dressing-gown aside to reveal a breast. The fifth man, a fifty-five-year-old redundant Accounts Supervisor, nodded and they went upstairs.

'You can fucking well get out, you scrubber.'
'Me get out, that's a laugh.'
'Laugh then.'
'Who pays the rent?'
'I said, laugh, damn you.'
'Who pays the gas?'
Richie picked up a threatening beer bottle.
'Who pays the electricity?'
'I mean it, I fucking warn you . . .'
'Who pays the . . .'
He threw the bottle.
'Where I come from a man can hit a girl with a bottle. They're real cricketers back home, not Aussie burks.'
'Where you come from they're niggers.'
'Racist, I just dunno what I think I'm doin', payin' rent for a racist, it's real demeaning.'
The fifth Mrs Richie Simpson put on a pink shift. Her new husband, all passion spent, sat with his head between his knees, brooding on his throwing in.
'Anyways,' she said, 'they'll be round for you soon.'
'Who?'
'How should I know who they'll be—in a van I guess,' she

laughed a warm southern laugh and went out to walk the streets.

She didn't in her Baptist heart approve of prostitution but it had occurred to her that it would be a good joke: to get Richie convicted for living on immoral earnings.

She had often been admired for her sense of humour.

Among other things.

'You doin' anything this evening?'

'Was it,' Atwater said, 'absolutely necessary to come here?'

'Not absolutely, but . . .'

'There are times when I feel I've had my fill of Indian restaurants. The nymphs, you might say, have departed; the rosebuds are faded. I have measured out my life in poppadums. To coin a phrase. Do you know, in my first year at Cambridge I must have eaten over a hundred prawn curries. The mind does a spot of boggling, eh? One trembles, yes? First-year men at Trinity—how it comes back—had to dine at six-thirty, which meant that night after night, being younger then, by ten o'clock I was starving. So across the road to the Taj Mahal . . . and inevitably, with what M. Arnold called the inevitability of great art, prawn curry . . . until finally one cracks, the day comes when one says, hold hard enough. I abjured. You lure me back again, you and Clare. *Drang nach Osten*, as you might say . . .'

'It would be fun to go to Cambridge, years since I've been there,' said a pink man Atwater had never identified. 'What do you think?'

'Cambridge, Cambridge . . .'

'Don't be so vague, Atwater.'

'It's a vague place . . . Fenland mists, hold you in a vice . . .'

'Oh well, vice, old boy, jolly old vice, nothing I always say like a spot of vice . . .'

'Another kettle of poisson . . .'

'Rum, how one seemed to have money then . . .'

'Goodness, Atwater, money, you?'

'Meant something in those days, at least I sometimes think it did . . .'

'So we come through fighting,' a voice boomed from beyond the partition where the room was even darker, 'Alabama comes through fighting . . .'

'Incredible . . . money,' Clare's tongue-tip touched her lower lip in wonder.

'*Laudator temporis acti*, that's what I'm in danger of turning into.'

'Atwater.'

'Yes?'

'It's not very polite to speak Latin, the waiters think you're discussing them . . .'

'So?'

'Just so.'

'I see . . .'

He nodded. Polly pressed her hand on his, submensally.

'Shall we,' she said, 'tell them?'

'Secrets . . .'

'Secrets . . .'

'Secrets . . . super . . .'

There seemed suddenly more girls than Atwater could account for.

'Oh goody, secrets . . .'

'I'm going to have a baby.'

'Polly.'

'Polly.'

'Atwater . . . you? Really? You . . . well I . . .'

Clare said: 'You really are snakes, utter snakiest snakes. Sweet though.'

'Smug, doesn't he look smug?'

'What else,' said Atwater, 'could I look?'

'Heels flying,' came the cry from beyond the partition, 'and irresistible, that's Alabama, boys . . .'

'Well, I never . . .'

'This calls for . . .'

'Champagne . . . *sans blague* . . .'

'That's the nub, now I come to think of it, of my objection,' Atwater gave a gloomy mumble, 'to Indian restaurants. Champagne and curry are not like Fortnum and Mason or Rogers and Astaire.'

A flat voice: 'Call me Mervyn, if you like . . .'

A shrill voice: 'But we must have champagne . . .'

A Russian voice: 'We do not need the curry . . . not at once . . .'

'Furthermore, I have observed that in Indian restaurants the champagne is rarely of a first-rate quality; that's how demoralising they are.'

Clare said, in an urgent undertone: 'Surely you should be carefullest, Polly, aren't things like champagne and curry bad for it?'

'You mustn't, ducky, call it "it", it's a creature. Anyway no, my doctor says, it's early days for that.'

A thin voice, from an angular girl who had once shared a flat with Clare and Polly: 'You mean you're actually going to have it.'

'Well, why not, Ruth, I can't imagine . . . it never crossed my mind for an instant not to . . .'

'Socially irresponsible . . .'

'Below the Mason-Dixon line,' came booming through, 'I want you-all to know we're more'n a country, we're an attitude of mind, a civilisation with traditions of human dignity . . .'

'Beazley a grandfather . . .'

'He can't be found . . .'

'He telephones . . . but they can't trace the calls . . .'

'What does your Mummy say, your Mama . . .?'

'Oh well you know Mummy . . .'

Mr Hedge pulled the nearest sleeve.

'So, you see, don't you, it's all right, it can't be true what she says in the diary, sick that's what it is, sick . . . tell me,' he added with a surge like waves on a desert beach, 'are you by any chance lubricious?'

'No.'

'Poor old Horridge though, that's what I say . . .'

'Come a cropper, sure as eggs is eggs.'

'But are they?'

'One wonders nowadays.'

'Guess we still think so in the CIA.'

'Interesting.'

'Want you-all to drink to the traditions of the Confederacy.'

'Cheers.'

'Money.'

'Talks . . . always talks.'

'So they say.'

'Oh but the Colonel's rich.'

'As Croesus.'

'Even Onassis.'

'Oh Atwater darling it's not true, he hasn't really a penny, poorest lamb, just likes to pretend.'

'Quite, quite, my dear.'

'Reverting to Horridge . . . I saw Harriet the other day, she hasn't heard from him either.'

'Well she wouldn't . . . that's a real tragic wasted woman, what a talent for being . . .'

'No, really I mean it . . . come up an' see me sometime . . .'

'Is that firm? Guess I'd better take a rain check . . .'

Atwater plucked Polly's sleeve.

'Who,' he said, 'are all these people?'

'Lots of them came out with me . . . but how they got here tonight . . .'

'God-guided doubtless . . . debs though, how quaint . . .'

'Lord bless my black and sinful soul . . . Mr Atwater . . .'

Atwater looked up. Aloysius stood there embracing the whole company with wide-stretched pastoral arms.

He proceeded to introduce his entourage . . .

'You all know this no-good catamite, this trendy Wilson, folks, and now this here white trash butch-poof Steve . . . on the run fro' the fuzz, he is, folks . . . Miss Polly, angel, I 'pologise for the company you find me in . . . *c'est la vie*, as they say in France, not so good, huh?'

'Jeremy baby,' Wilson advanced on the young lawyer, hands a-flutter . . .

'Hi, Jer,' Steve spoke without lip movement.

'Jeremy, do you really . . .'

'Clients of mine, clients, just clients . . .'

'Well really, most familiar, not I take it from Shropshire.'

'One can't be sure, that one has a certain *je ne sais quoi*.'

'Surely not . . .'

'No, no, the white one, a touch of your actual Shropshire lads there, wouldn't you . . .'

Aloysius mounted a chair, champagne in hand.

'This news is good news, Massa Atwater. Folks, I give you de baby. Drink up.'

He inclined towards Atwater, almost toppling over in deference.

'Mass' Atwater, that position now, you'll be needin' more'n a valet, man, even, Lord help us, a maitred hotel. Aloysius is in de market, sure thing.'

'You sure is pretty, Mervyn baby . . .'

'Really, you think so, Mr Wilson . . . strange, it's a long time since . . .'

'An' lonesome too, I guess, no life bein' a politician's boy, I know . . . me an' Stevie now, we got plans for you . . .'

'CIA did you say, extraordinary chap I know . . .'

'What's the name . . .?'

'Ngunga . . .'

'Funny sort of name, not British.'

'A recommendation surely these days.'

'When's it due, have you thought of a name?'

'Well we did think of Fred . . . only thing my brother had a bull-terrier called Fred, a psychopath.'

'Seth, sure I've heard him referred to as Dr Seth . . .'

'CIA or KGB, it's a toss-up these days.'

'Who can tell?' Atwater leant confidentially towards the pink speaker. 'He is like the Mona Lisa, older than the rocks.'

'Golly.'

'Yes, sir, you-all gotta come see Alabama . . . I'm Alabama bound.'

Much later, after long travel, ennui, love, and what seemed like slaughter, when the tablecloth was saffron stained, the bottles emptied, brandy glasses sticky and some even of the girls had departed, in taxis, mist or their lovers' arms, Atwater found himself clutching a piece of paper.

'This bill,' he spoke flatly, 'is, even accounting for the arabesques of Oriental imagery, impossible.'

A large dark hand descended.

'You jus' leave it to ol' Aloysius . . . hey there, Gunga Din.'

IV

Adolf stood in the concourse of Victoria Station, sweating. This wasn't only because of the fur-lined overcoat he was unseasonably wearing. It was a garment he considered suitable to the image he now had of trains, the result of a poor memory and too many viewings of his favourite movie, Garbo's *Anna Karenina*. Mental agitation however played a bigger part than physical discomfort in his condition. Stevie had gone to buy the tickets, sullenly and reluctantly, and hadn't come back yet.

'Why the fuck are you going to fucking Brighton?'

'I've told you, ducky, time and again, it's duty.'

Stevie's jaw had dropped and a look Adolf feared entered his eye; it was easy to make the poor lamb feel you were laughing at him.

Now the fear that he mightn't return was added, Ossa on Pelion-like, to Adolf's terror at being out of his subterranean lair. It was the first time he'd left it in three years. Life was organised there on his own terms.

'Still,' he'd said to Stevie patting his cheek, 'I've got no choice, see. The Colonel and me, we're blood brothers.'

'Christ, at your age.'

'It's what we've been through together.'

'Pathetic, it really is . . .'

Adolf had smiled, bravely.

But he felt his courage disintegrating here, where everyone was staring at him, knowing him for what he was, an old poof, a capon, a queen, and despising him accordingly. They might start throwing things or spitting soon.

His feet hurt too in unaccustomed leather.

The station was full of rozzers. They couldn't help seeing the boy. He shouldn't have allowed him to come.

'S'pose you want me to hold your hand, Christ, what a . . .'

A good faithful boy, really, good as he'd ever had.

'You know what you look like, don't you?'

'Oooh I didn't see you, you've taking your time, I was anxious, that's what, anxious.'

'Well, there was this smashing piece gave me the old eye . . .'

'What a one you are . . .'

Adolf's relief was making him giggly . . .

'Anything you fancy before we go?'

'Well . . .'

'What a one you are.'

Colonel Beazley turned the telegram over and over in his hand, as if estimating its value. Then he added it to the pile on the bedside table and turned his attention to the sea again. There must have been a dozen telegrams, all unopened, in the pile. Outside on the front, he could see the Boy and girl leaning on the sea-rail. Abandoned newspapers swirled around their ankles.

Colonel Beazley picked up the telephone. 'Send me a chicken sandwich and a bottle of Krug,' he snapped. (You can tell a man by the style of his breakdown.) 'And leave them outside my door as usual.'

He took a ten-pound note from his dressing-gown pocket and stood ready to slip it under the door when he heard the waiter bring the tray. Then he waited again till the footsteps receded before opening the door and furtively drawing in the tray.

He sat down by the telephone again and began to dial. He listened to the bell ringing in the lonely house in Norfolk and was aware of the echo sounding to the beach and out into the grey wastes of sea. For years he had tried to talk to his wife, now only the bell sounded. It was like blank verse.

The girl had turned from the sea-rail. She was holding her palm outstretched before her. A crucifix was revealed. The Colonel watched a blob of saliva form on the Boy's thin lips.

A party of Japanese tourists stopped and began photographing madly. The spittle was arrested. A plane flew low overhead. A brown and white pigeon landed on the windowsill and fixed its gaze on the Colonel. He banged on the glass. It cocked its head. He bit into the chicken sandwich.

Dr Ngunga trudged up the hillside in the mist. Many would have repined. It was all to begin again. Seth Ngunga knew himself to be undaunted. Even the accounts his emissaries had brought him of Horridge's condition, his seemingly complete collapse, were only to be regarded as a challenge.

As he climbed he sang a hymn,

> 'Yield not to temptation
> For yielding is sin.
> Shun evil companions
> Bad language disdain . . .'

He curled his upper lip on the word disdain. The hymn had been a favourite at the Mission School. The precepts had stuck. Dr Ngunga's language was old-fashioned in its purity, like the polish on the button-boots he wore in town.

He came to the refuge. It had been built for hikers, then abandoned by popular demand and boarded up; it had become apparent that the provision of mountain refuges encouraged the rash and inexperienced to venture on the hills and, unwary, die there. The reflection caused the doctor to nod sagely. There were analogies in politics.

Horridge didn't answer his knock. Ngunga pushed the door open. A lesser man would have been afraid. Horridge was sitting at a rough deal table, his shirt undone. A scrub of beard disguised his chin and his eyes were filmed. A black bottle and a squat glass stood at his right hand. He gave no greeting to his old friend but raised the glass, emptied it, banged it on the table and stretched his hand to the whisky. The movement was arrested by Dr Ngunga's sudden grasping of his wrist.

'Horridge,' said the doctor, 'this is not the end for you.'

His voice was low and musical.

'You have been deceived,' said the doctor, 'well, it is the lot of man. Even when we see with certainty, when we walk with history, which is destiny, and are conscious of it, our achievement is never what we have envisaged in our aim. Think of that.'

Horridge gave no sign that he had heard. His fingers still reached for the bottle, their petrified aspiration the most urgent thing in the room.

It was lit by a single kerosene lamp.

Outside a wind was rising, from the north-east, coming across the moors.

'Do you remember,' asked Dr Ngunga, 'what they meant by soul?'

His finger registered the unchanging beat of Horridge's pulse.

'We who walk with history know better than to talk of the soul. It is dead as the God it imaged.'

'Christ,' said Horridge.

'But then,' said Dr Ngunga, aware that Horridge was stirring but giving no sign that he had observed it, 'there is, we know, no death. Death, too, is dead. Biology teaches us that. There is merely cessation, transformation and, comrade, this soul we see to be merely our myth of ourselves. That is what is vital. Your myth is, for the moment, the brief moment, obscured. I have come to bring you vision. I am the resurrection.'

A long shudder passed through Horridge's body,

> 'Burke's the butcher, Hare's the thief,
> Knox the boy who buys the beef.'

The words came out in a reluctant sing-song, autonomously, grinding.

'We're the resurrection men, is that it?' he said and tossed back his head and laughed.

'Pardon me,' said Dr Ngunga, 'I do not see the joke. It is how modern man came to know the science of anatomy.'

.　　.　　.　　.　　.

Adolf had had difficulty on the train. He had been upset to discover that there were no longer carriages with compartments where you could pull the blinds down and travel in genteel seclusion. He hadn't liked the way a stout lady dressed in purple had looked at him and Stevie and boomed:

'It makes me sick, damned sick. Flaunting that's what it is, I said flaunting. Sodom and Gomorrah also ran.'

'Don't you worry,' whispered a nice little black girl eager to reassure Adolf, 'she goes on like this every Thursday, it's her pension day.'

That hadn't pleased Adolf. No doubt she intended to be kind, but it was no business of hers. Shouldn't be in the country either, little slut.

'You needn't bother,' Stevie said, 'he's a racist this one, he don't like spades.'

'And why should he,' cried the purple lady, quite excited, 'is the gentleman paid to . . .?'

'Are you?' said a timid clergyman, anxious to do good works but ignorant of the means.

''Course he isn't.'

'It's a proper scandal, that's what . . .'

'You can't expect him to . . .'

'Not if he isn't paid . . .'

'The labourer is worthy . . .'

'One way of putting it but the way I see it granting mind you as you must thinking economic trendwise in the climate of this moment in time . . .'

'I'm not paid, I do it free . . .'

'That's your way, the amateur touch it's called . . .'

'Admirable . . .'

'Most . . .'

'Rhubarb I say . . .'

'Quite quite . . .'

'Don't think I don't admire you, sir, it's a rare treat to come across nowadays but still viewed critically, eagle-eyewise, must admit in every field the day of the amateur's over, fini . . .'

'Got a point there . . . Peter May the last . . . shan't look on . . . not again . . .'

'So what I say is, the gentleman doesn't like our coloured friends, he isn't paid to like them, no dispute there, but shouldn't he be, that's the nub . . .'

'Oh very nubular . . .'

'Getting down to the nitty-gritty . . .'

'Bloody nonsense, might as well pay me to like pansies . . .'

'Why not, why not? Just as sensible as some of the things they pay . . .'

'More I'd say . . .'

'Far far better thing . . .'

'You see . . .'

'Directors of Leisure, f'instance . . .'

'With you there . . .'

Atwater and Polly were walking in Hyde Park. It was years since Atwater had done more than skirt it. In his late twenties he had often spent wet autumn afternoons to the smell of smoking leaves, his eyes searching through the rising mists for the impressionable shapes of girls in macintoshes. He had never dared, or even chosen, to approach such a girl, but had followed her, in others' eyes furtively, but to himself with a gentle lyricism, until leaving the park she had been swallowed up in the crowds, walking out of his imagination back into the city. It was more satisfactory when she left by Marble Arch, headed for Oxford Street.

Now he and Polly walked together instead, occasionally touching.

'I remember . . .'

'What?'

'Nothing . . . the thieving movements of time . . .'

Only when Polly stood in careless attitudes was the child's growth within her apparent. Atwater was glad it was still secret. Sometimes he placed his finger on her belly.

'Like a fig ripening . . .'

'On a south-facing wall . . . where are we going to live, I've been thinking about that . . . ?'

'Oh yes . . .'

'I don't like it when you say "oh yes".'

'We might get married . . .'

'Atwater . . .'

'In the eyes of God we are married . . . or so they say . . . you're not a Catholic?'

'C of E . . .'

'It might make me uncomfortable to marry a Catholic, intensity round a potential corner . . .'

'You really mean it . . . marriage . . . why not . . . ?'

'Oh yes,' Atwater said.

It diverted attention, he hoped, from the housing problem. It was the third time Polly had mentioned it. He found nothing wrong with her flat himself, apart from Mr Hedge's presence of course.

'They wouldn't let us in the Turkish Baths, you see, and anyway I don't expect the atmosphere would be right for this thing,' she touched her belly.

'Oh no.'

'So I've been wondering . . . is there any of your grand-mother's money left?'

'I really couldn't say. Jeremy's become very furtive. I expect he's embezzled it, lawyers usually do.'

'Because I thought we could use it as a deposit . . .'

'I suppose he's being blackmailed, poor chap. There was a lift-boy called Benny, stands to reason, wouldn't you say?'

'You see, I thought we should buy something . . .'

'Buy . . .'

Atwater felt a cold claw of fear in his gut . . . to buy was to enter areas he had forsworn . . . hadn't fatherhood though already taken him through the gateway that led from the desert of the streets (where all the devils were familiars) to the walled garden? He looked round him wildly. He said to himself again, 'the daring isolation of men who are not in prison'; only it didn't seem quite right.

'It's cheaper to buy . . .'

'It doesn't seem so . . .'

'In the long run . . .'

'In the long run we're dead . . .'

'It's not the Marathon.'

He saw it coming. In a moment she would say and now she said:

'You'll have to get a job, I know it's awful . . .'

'Rilke said, a job was like death without the dignity of death. It's a hard thing to say but I'm with Rilke.'

'There's Social Security of course but they won't give us a mortgage unless you've got a job . . .'

'Even if his name was Rainer Maria . . . are you sure?'

'Yes, I checked.'

'But you have a job.'

'Saving the country, I know, but somehow I don't think that's going to last much longer . . .'

'Past saving of course, Mrs Hedge however . . .'

'That's it. I think she's going to prefer a secretary who hasn't got a big belly . . . I told you how she feels about the Virgin.'

Atwater said, 'I'm unemployable, it's well known, it's almost a tourist attraction I'm so unemployable.'

'Darling . . .'

'Oh God . . .'

Phantasmagoric images loomed before him, black and lurid. He groaned, startling a nearby duck which dived for shelter.

'What could I do?'

'You're so clever.'

'It's the wrong sort of cleverness.'

'I suppose, it sounds awful I know, but couldn't you teach?'

Atwater grasped at a passing straw. 'Not with my prison record.'

'In London I've been told that's positively an advantage. You might become a headmaster straight away.'

'No, no . . .'

'You're probably too old for advertising.'

'It's a young man's trade,' Atwater spoke happily. This was a step in the right direction. He was prepared to co-operate at length in a discussion of what he couldn't do. Lesser men, with a feebler grip on their personal myth, might find such talk distressing and diminishing; not Atwater.

'It's no good,' he said, giving the ball a vigorous boot. 'Considering any of the professions that, however half-wittedly, demand a period of training.'

'No, and I don't suppose they'd relish training you . . .'

'These are harsh words.'

'But true . . .'

'Undoubtedly.'

'Don't look so smug.'

'That's true too. As a child I was often accused of looking smug. So you see there's not much left. I don't think I could labour, not at any rate in a manner worthy of hire.'

'You know about antiques, don't you?'

'Very little.'

Polly looked sad. It was her fate always only to be able to feel for those incapable of helping themselves; there were moments when she saw herself as a spiritual soup-kitchen. Her lip trembled. Atwater, seeing it, sighed . . . if only people would see that all survival was internal. He said, 'There's always Aloysius, he wants to give me a job, you know . . .'

The sea-gulls flew squawking round the Boy and girl. The Boy was now speaking hard at the girl. Colonel Beazley knew that her wrist was being scored by the Boy's nails. Her face however didn't register the pain she must surely feel; her whole heritage told her she could only endure. The Colonel put down the field-glasses through which he had been gazing at them and nodded. The ignorant instinct of the lower animals. Suicide meant enough self-realisation to be aware of disgust. That, rather than hopelessness, was its true cause. He thought of his wife; to be able no longer to go on. Her affair with Horridge was a dramatisation of her self-disgust.

A taxi drew up before the hotel. Its door opened. Great buttocks emerged. A moment of jellied wobbling, the figure straightened and the Colonel recognised Adolf.

'Great Scott.'

Stevie followed and began arguing with the driver. He handed over some money and they turned towards the hotel door. The Colonel listened to the silence, heard it broken by their feet on the stairs and knock at his door, was aware of its resumption, then shattered it himself.

It was some moments before Adolf could speak. The Colonel with old-world, practised courtesy settled him in a chair, told Stevie to go first to Hell then for a yoghourt.

'You'll be surprised to see me, Colonel.'

'Certainly not. Who else?'

'Ah . . .'

'Realised it had to be you . . .'

'Only thing is, sir, don't know what I've got to say. Only just felt I'd got to come. Dare say you can make something of that.'

'Oh yes, absolutely. Look, Adolf old fruit, you see those two out there, the Boy and the girl?'

'Dishy, definitely dishy, not safe, mind you, but definitely dishy.'

'Yes, yes, put that bloody yoghourt down and get the hell out of here, told you before . . .'

'Do what Colonel says, dearie, he's in charge, always is . . .'

'That's better, can't think why you cart him about with you, Adolf, doesn't seem to have any proper filial sentiment, mind you I don't know where you'll find it nowadays, makes me glad I haven't got a son.'

Adolf uncapped the yoghourt. (Stevie should know he didn't fancy the banana one, but maybe it was all the poor lamb could find.)

'You were saying, Colonel, that Boy . . .'

'And girl, I've been watching them, days on end, they're

114

always there. Do you see them? Do you see the dark circles of their eyes? Do you see what is in their eyes? It makes me afraid.'

'Colonel,' said Adolf, 'there's one thing you leave out of that. I've come to see you. I've left the Club first time in I don't know when, it frightened me, you know, but that's what I've done. You don't see that in their eyes now do you? Or the things we learnt in the desert.'

'But it might be all mirages, that's what I fear.'

'Colonel, I'm here . . . not in imagination. I know the horrors too but here I am. Let me show you something.'

He drew a battered photograph from his breast pocket. It showed a young man looking like a cheap imitation of T. E. Lawrence sitting on a camel so aged it might well have belonged to Lawrence. He looked at it a moment, then put it in front of the Colonel. Beazley's bloodshot eyes became moist. He took a sip of champagne, then another.

'Long time ago,' he said.

'But I've always carried it. That proves something, don't it, that we reach out beyond ourselves?'

The Colonel picked up his field-glasses again and fixed them on the Boy and girl.

'The Japs come and watch 'em too, taking snaps. Don't know what it means, but it's significant, no doubt about it.'

Mrs Hedge was in a temper. She hadn't seen Polly for two weeks. Her husband hadn't yet returned. She was having to take the Pekingese out herself at night because the detective said it was more than his life was worth to go out on his own after dark. He had enemies, he muttered. Anyway he was often drunk by dusk. She had tried to have him replaced but the Home Secretary had not been co-operative.

'You don't realise,' he said, 'how lucky you are to have a grown-up detective. Some of us are having to make do with school-leavers.'

'But that distorts the unemployment figures.'

'Exactly.'

'I shall put down a question about it.'

Now she had received a letter from Polly saying she was going to get married. It was too much. She called MacGilchrist, her detective.

'There is a man called Atwater,' she said.

'Never heard of him.'

'I want him put in the forefront of the battle.'

MacGilchrist sat down heavily without being asked. He was a stout man of low morale who never felt comfortable standing, except at a bar counter.

'You must be joking,' he said.

Mrs Hedge's eyes flashed blue steel (as political correspondents were wont to say when she was angered).

'I have no time to joke,' she said, 'I am a public figure. This Atwater is a subversive. I felt it from the first. I want you to investigate him. I want the dirt.'

MacGilchrist sighed. There were people who had a misconception of the Police. The higher up you got, the more you found it.

'And what would he have done?'

'That is for you to establish. I want him down.'

MacGilchrist shook his head.

'It's not on,' he said.

'You mean you're really going to get married. Goodness. Does Atwater know?'

'He mentioned the word, I mean, he said it first.'

'Goodness . . . Polly?'

'Yes.'

'He knows what it means?'

'Yes.'

'Goodness. What about Horridge?'

'Horridge is in the past.'

'Yes but the past, you know, Polly, the past isn't something over and done with.'

'Clare, what do you mean? You're not becoming metaphysical, are you?'

'Can't say, really, I've been feeling strangest. Perhaps I am. But I'm back on the pill so it may just be that . . . who can tell, ducky?'

'Does that mean Jeremy's . . .'

'Oh no, poorest Jeremy.'

'What do you mean? What's happened?'

'Well, Jeremy, no.'

'Uncle Giles then?'

'Past it, poor love.'

'Well?'

'You are persistent. Just in case actually.'

'I see . . . Clare, you haven't heard of Horridge, have you?'

'Not a squeak, not a bat's squeak.'

'It's very strange really the way he's just vanished . . . I know Mummy's hoping still . . . personally I don't care if he's in the Grand Union Canal . . . how is Jeremy anyway?'

'Schizophrenic poorest.'

'How sad, why this time?'

'Still the same really, Shropshire on his left, the gay life in the red corner, too too . . .'

'Never mind. Well, I must . . .'

'Don't ring off, ever so cosy, what are you wearing?'

'Nothing.'

'Polly.'

'Nudo, or rather, nuda.'

'Are you often, at home I mean . . .'

'Well I like it specially when I telephone, only thing is, have to be careful because we've still got Mervyn here you know.'

'I had an idea about Mervyn.'

'No?'

'Yes, Harriet I thought . . .'

'Horridge's wife? Atwater used to say she spent all her time in a dressing-gown. I don't think that would do for Mervyn, he needs livening up you know. Still sweet of you to think, keep trying.'

'Tell you who I met last night. That frightful man, I don't know his name. The one who says he's a novelist and

Atwater's a character in his novel. He frightens me rather. What if he's right? Oh, Polly, I am sorry, I could kick myself, how tactless, forget I said it, anyway it's crazy . . .'

'Oh yes, it's crazy,' said Polly but she wondered because it was well known that what was crazy could still be true all the same and this was indeed the case time and time again.

'How's your father, you know I had a thought about your father, would you like to hear?'

'Oh yes, he's in Brighton though.'

'It wasn't really a thought, a dream actually, very strange, very sexy . . . we were whoring, your papa and me, in a gondola no less . . .'

'He would be flattered.'

'I seem to be turning into the sort of girl who fancies oldies, I'd never have thought it. Of course they've always fancied me, you too of course, but me terrifically, so maybe it's just that I'm getting nicer. How's Mrs Hedge, you're her type exactly natch.'

'I'm not pleased with Mrs Hedge, not at all pleased.'

'Why not?'

'She's been setting Special Branch on Atwater.'

'Goodness.'

The lift ascended, too fast for Atwater. He was wearing, at Polly's insistence, an unaccustomed suit.

'Smart but not sporty's the calculated effect. We don't want you looking half-asleep either.'

He rubbed his back on the lift wall trying to make the suit look as though he had slept in it. It came from the Colonel's wardrobe. Polly had appropriated several.

'He used to go crazy buying suits, I don't think he's bought any for a long time now, poor lamb, but there's lots to choose from.'

'Oh good.'

The one he wore was in Prince of Wales check.

'It looks versatile, what we want.'

'I ought to have a watch-chain.'

'Don't be silly.'

'And a bowler hat.'

'No, we want you to look contemporary.'

'Bowler hats aren't contemporary.'

'Not at all.'

'What makes you think suits are?'

The lift stopped at the thirteenth floor. Atwater, flicking a furtive one up and down the corridor, emerged. A flashing sign read 'Executive Personnel'. He stepped on the mat. The light flashed green. Letters sprang into being.

'Come right in,' they read, in capitals.

It wasn't an office that could have accommodated many personnel, even midgets. The man with gap teeth who lay in the chair behind the desk was already sufficiently small. He didn't remove his feet from its top. There was a transfer of a naked lady on the right sole; she was swinging from a trapeze, upside down. The dwarf waved a tiny, excessively manicured paw. Atwater sat down. The dwarf placed a finger on a red button and pushed.

'Watch the birdie,' he said.

The television screen that dominated the south wall at once showed a copy of the form Polly had made Atwater fill in.

'Neat, i'n't it?'

'Couldn't you just have . . .?'

'Processed it's been, got some gaps in your CV you have.'

Atwater nodded, impassive, a statue, the imperturbable.

'Filleminwillya.'

'I beg your . . .'

'Whatyabindointhen . . .'

'Ah . . .'

Well, he'd warned Polly it would come to this.

'I had,' he explained, 'independent means. They have now evaporated. So I need a job.'

'Gabbitas Thring.'

'I'm sorry?'

'Thems for those what have evaporated IM.'

'I have no wish to teach. Indeed I shudder, repelled.'

'Workers we want. Personnel executive, executive personnel supply, eager beavers. Face it, Mr A, what can you do?'

The dwarf waggled a foot.

'Face it, look at the screen, Mr Atwater, give it me, you can't do nothing, exactly nothing.'

'Exactly.'

'That's better, that's the stuff, so tell you what, Mr Atwater, I'll help you. There's no jobs, out-of-date concept that's what it is. We're interested in an employment situation. Look at me.'

He swung his boots off the desk and leered at Atwater.

'I'm not what you think I am.'

'No,' said Atwater.

'So what can we do wiv you, can't do nothing, can we now, not after you've come all the way to see me, on a Wednesday too. Been in the nick, 'ave you?'

'Well . . . briefly.'

'Attaboy.'

Atwater was charmed by the open generosity of the chap's smile. It suggested candour.

'Often the way wiv IM. How'd you like to do sumpin in the hush-hush line maybe?'

'Not at all.'

'O.K., hush-hush a bye baby, no go education, only leaves the telly.'

'Is there nothing you can do to help me?'

'Sorry, cocky, the rest's jobs see? Honest sweat.'

'Executives?'

'This moment in time, day and age like, even executives sweat. Creates a market for deodorants. Oiling the wheels of commerce some call it . . . Mr Atwater why've you come here?'

'Why do you think? Why does anyone come here?'

'Let's not play games. How's we stop playing games?'

Atwater frowned. 'You baffle me.'

'O.K., O.K., O.K., baby, play it that way. For me you're a checker, legit is as legit does, baby.'

'Really I'm afraid.'

'O.K. I've stretched a few . . . but you can't say I offered you anything I can't supply, fair's fair, fair do's . . .'

'It's no wonder,' Atwater said to Polly, 'there are a million and a half unemployed with recruiting officers like that.'

V

Mrs Hedge made a speech to the nation. She said there were
drones at work undermining the nation's vitality. She said
there were skulkers, those who would not put their hand to
the wheel, who sought to reap where they had not sown.
That lets us out, said Atwater. Sh, said Polly. Me anyway,
said Atwater, I've been doing the sowing. You are conceited,
Polly said, and it's getting worse. Mrs Hedge went on to
state emphatically that the situation was deteriorating hourly.
Even those who had been doing honest work had despaired
or been corrupted by the pervasive laxity. The Government
was pulling the wool over its own eyes, let alone the people's.
The Prime Minister watching TV as he lay in his steaming
bath (which he had decided some time back was a good place
from which to contemplate the decline and fall) began to
giggle. Harriet Horridge having happened to hit on this
station while vainly searching for Blues sung by Billie Holli-
day pulled her dressing-gown tighter. Mrs Hedge had once
been her Philosophy tutor. They had discussed Idealism and
Bishop Berkeley. Harriet put her elbows on the table, unsure
of its existence. Mrs Hedge embarked on further flights of
excoriation. Colonel Beazley in his Brighton hotel contemplated the front deserted in the half-moonlight by all but the
Boy and the girl. He hearkened to Mrs Hedge. Words
formed on his frothy lips: mene, mene, tekel, upharsin. An
interviewer like a fawning spaniel was now speaking to Mrs
Hedge. He asked her if we could take it that her policy would
be painful. It will bite here and there, she smilingly said. Unfortunately, remarked Atwater, her hands are suddenly invisible so of where and where we remain alas ignorant. Dr
Ngunga sitting in the lounge of a Station Hotel somewhere
in the West where trains no longer ran rubbed his hands,
found a pink one belonging to a strawberry blonde typist had
unbeknownst interpolated itself betwixt his, and, ever-re-

sourceful, carried it to his lips. God is working his purpose out, he whispered. You are naughty, she said, keep it in. Never, said Mrs Hedge, her wit bristling, had so much been owed by so few to so many. The Prime Minister extended the toes of his left foot and twiddled the hot tap blissfully. That's rather clever, Clarici, Jeremy said, you know that's really rather good. Only Conservative freedom can work, said Mrs Hedge. You don' find me votin' Socialist, man, ain't a gentleman's party, tha's a fac', announced Aloysius. You really fin' that yo' experience, Mervyn baby, sure Conservative freedom work swell fo' you, better with Wilson, babyman, youz gettin' prettier ev'ry day, youz a Liberal at heart, Mervyn baby. Mrs Hedge remarked with demure candour that nevertheless she would not be daunted by the magnitude of the task. Never be daunted, Atwater said, secret of my success, never been daunted, what about a spot more gin. In the Norfolk vastwastes Lady Gertrude strode over a windmill-bespattered heath, Great Danes at her heels and transistor to her ear. She was unable to find any relevance in Mrs Hedge's oration. She strained her ear for reference to Horridge, who, almost uniquely, did not hear the speech.

Night fell darker. Fog crept up the river. There was public silence.

Atwater and Polly lay in bed linked but for a long time quiet.

He thought: and so . . . we go on . . . towards satiety then what but the future every bullet has its billet red sails in the sunset dies in the west where Arthur and I hope hope there is still the silence of . . . sticky hand and a crust forms on the thigh cramp just a right arm sorry cramp out of the window we came down in the lift sublime to that is journey from not wanted on the wilder shores of love poozing and bosing girls different species much as sex live by a different timescale Bergson has it fog on the Kentish heights live with my son soon go through with more her than me least I can list lips and Polly marriage has many pains but celibacy has no pleasures Stendhal never married though gin agin once upon a time there was a man who never felt anything and had gone quite numb being numb he could fall off roofs without fear and mene people found this very impressive he could and did wake up in a cell and run his fingers down the wet tiles and say well boys here we are again he could see old women run over in the street and say you've got to keep nimble chaps wits about you so what about another just in case sometimes he was aware that he had gone numb and he could always account for it as a super self-defence inscrutable too he was originally so sensitive he had to go numb or scream it was much easier being numb than screaming though though sometimes had to admit it in the dead hours when cocks crew in the country and only taxis in the city streets then voices penetrated the numbness and a cold trickle of sweat than through the formed enseamed crust and Polly said:

'Atwater . . . are we going anywhere . . . you're not asleep?'

'Asleep? I never sleep in bed.'

'No, Atwater it all suddenly seems empty.'

He put his hand on her belly.

'It's a night thought,' he said.

'I know. Night thoughts.'

'Different winter thoughts.'

'Seem to mean more.'

He moved his hand down from her belly into softness and thought: what am I doing here consoling one way of looking another might be disarming shield lies rusting in the wet woods and living.

'Can you imagine it's come to this, this room and the world dead?'

'Bigger than I've thought it, lets you in and this.'

The strawberry blonde whose name was Kim said to Dr Ngunga, 'If my mother could see me.'

'Ah,' he said, 'it's an afflicting thought—motherhood, the sacred state we hide everything from.'

'It's Kim Novak I'm called after.'

'And pretty as a picnic you are.'

'My old man'd larrup me,' she said, 'oooh fuck me again.'

'Libenter liberaliterque.'

Horridge wrote: 'Political action is in the ultimate sense merely the kinetic expression of the Will. It realises the *Weltanschauung* of the Unconscious. It is the Fantasia of the Overdrive. A tepid inner man will find utterance in a muddy liberalism, a canting social democracy, a constipated conservatism that dare not openly avow the class basis that fundamentally sustains it.

But all this is the evening of the nineteenth century. It is decadence.

Existential man knows that the barriers he erects are not prescribed by any morality other than that he has made for himself.

Social democracy resembles bourgeois marriage. It is a retreat from the yawning void of naked existence.'

Atwater turned over in the bed. Polly was asleep. Her breathing had a vulnerable rhythm. His heart was cramped, his will gripped, monstrous shades, the demon of the stairs again, it is the cause, also the curse. Thy flesh is as my flesh. His hand could not advance to touch Polly in self-consolation. Meanwhile, she breathed, in a common bed. Night thoughts are black in the rooky wood. To partake of the Colonel's agony, exactly that, consents to death but conquers agony. Eyeless in Gaza, the vulgar only scaped who stood without. Atwater in the blanket of the dark found himself pierced . . . the nature of solitude, illusion of conversation . . . now might I do it pat.

Polly, he knew, was dreaming. She gave a little squirm and a sigh. Polly's dreams were of green boskage and yellow fields, dog-roses in English hedgerows, October stubble, the orderly procession of the seasons, pheasant from October to January, gun-dogs questing in the coverts, the sun setting low behind the church's Saxon tower, the Roman wall growing in the dusk. There were rabbits in her dreams and the dust was rich.

Atwater though fished more often by the gasworks than in streams where the trout rose to the may-fly.

Atwater got up and padded through to the kitchen. He sat by the window and lit a cigarette. The smoke rose straight as from a sacrifice. You are being trained to accept responsibility. It is in your bones. You have a lie in your bones. Rum, said Atwater, speaking aloud and deciding to open a bottle of wine. Very rum. Cheap white wine was an answer. Castelli Romani with a plastic cork. The silence here was different from the silence in the Turkish bath. There the murmurs of guilt were inaudible. He drank half a tumbler of wine. Sour, invigorating and, in sufficient quantity, drunk-making.

The child, his as well as Polly's, was growing . . .

As the Governor of North Carolina said to the Governor of South Carolina . . .

What's done cannot be . . .

In my beginning is my . . .

Birth, copulation and death . . .

Story of my life give or take a glass or two.

'I is promiscuous Jerry baby an' I glories in it.'

'Yes, but really, Wilson . . .'

'What's more, I'se gettin' Mervyn roun' to ma way of thinkin', ain't tha' so, Mervyn baby?'

'Wouldn't like you think . . .'

'Wilson you oughta listen to ol' Aloysius, you is leadin' a dangerous life, full o' peril. You jist cast the glory o' yo' eye on ma good frien' Richie an' you can see the rewards the good Lord has in store fo' them that cannot bridle their sexual appetites. Tha' man is on the slippery slope tha's bedecked wiv primroses. There's adders there too an' serpents.'

'You bin an' got religion, Aloysius?'

'I gotta spirit. I gotta spirit right here an' when I'se moved by that spirit I gotta proclaim . . .'

'Dickie Nixon, we'se a comin' to the world's end. How long yo' give us, Aloysius baby?'

'Yo', Wilson, I give less time than it takes a yaller sprintin' colt to cover five furlongs.'

'We gotta be quick Jer baby.'

Atwater was travelling on the Inner Circle. He had already been round twice. Occasionally, at Sloane Square for instance, he stopped off for a drink. He was reading 'The Londoner's Log' in an *Evening Standard* abandoned by an Arab. The Londoner revealed that Mrs Hedge would be spending part of the Recess at a Retreat near Barking. Atwater was sceptical, as of all Anglo-Catholic information. Also he had once known a man, a dismal fornicator, who worked on the Diary. The knowledge had not aided credulity. He lit a cigarette and looked up. The same—or at least a similar (for vice marks its own resemblances)—fornicator was sitting opposite him.

Atwater tapped the paragraph with a moody forefinger.

'Did you write this?'

'I severed my connection.'

'I doubt the truth of this paragraph.'

'Sure.'

It was a word which sat uneasily on his lips.

'So I thought of you.'

'Where are you going, Atwater?'

'Around.'

'It's been a long time.'

'It has.'

'Since we met, I mean.'

'My meaning too.'

'They tell me you're getting married.'

'Who? Me?'

'You.'

'Things people say.'

'Would be a laugh.'

'Would it?'

'Sure. Just when everyone is through Atwater catches up.'

'You could put it like that.'

'I'm on my third. Extra-curricular activities too, goes without saying.'

'It couldn't, not with you.'

'What?'

'Go without saying.'

Changing his plans Atwater rose and left the train at the next station. He crossed the platform to resume his journey in the opposite direction. He had been at Prep School with that man. Hard to feel. Another life. Meanwhile what he had said . . . Atwater looked at the advertisements.

There was no doubt which of them was in tune.

Richie was arrested at half-past two in the morning. Information had been laid that he was living on immoral earnings.

'Don't like your sort,' said the first policeman rubbing his hands.

'What's it worth to change your opinion?'

The policeman brought his knee up casually into Richie's groin.

'Look, Cyril,' he said to his companion, 'he's been took bad.'

'Oh call a doctor, Vivian.'

'No need, he's straightening up.'

'He's tough this one for a ponce.'

'Even ponces come all sorts up to a point.'

'You got it wrong,' Richie whined, 'you got it all wrong. Immoral earnings, Christ mate, the alimony I pay, immoral earnings with the alimony I pay, shit. Four sheilas I pay alimony to, maybe five, Christ, I'm a hero of the sex war.'

'Listen to the man, Cyril.'

'I'm listening, Vivian.'

'Fair makes your heart bleed.'

'Or your gums, Vivian.'

'Hearken, Aussie,' Cyril said, 'you're a loser. So you're paying alimony? So what? You know what that makes you? That makes you a pimp.'

'An exploiter of female frailty,' Vivian said. 'You're facilitating the committal of fornication. Call it sex. That's a sin. You're an *agent provocateur*, that's what.'

'You're anything we care to make it. Vivian's a Catholic, I'm a Marxist. We can't tolerate unbridled sexual appetites any more. We put the reins on. Alimony, that's just a bribe; it's an investment in adultery. Hey, Vivian, he's a *rentier* too.'

'And a usurer. Usury's a sin. Letting out women at interest.'

'Your wife walks the street.'

'That's an inducement to sex.'

'Holds back productivity.'

'You need correction.'

'Corrective training.'

'Spiritual re-education.'

'We got you by the balls, Aussie, left and right.'

'I don't get you,' Richie said, 'you ain't ordinary coppers.'

'There are no ordinary coppers.'

'Nevermore.'

'We must ask you to come down to the Centre.'

Horridge had moved higher up the mountain. He was now living in a cave. He had grown a beard. He spent the day lying in skins at the far end of the cavern. At night he emerged to the opening and looked at the stars. He no longer wrote. Instead he remembered.

There was a penthouse in Manhattan where a Jewish

lady lived. Three walls were clear glass and the fourth a mirror. Horridge had co-habited there for two months. She was a very exquisite lady, dressed by Balmain. At night they played backgammon. She sometimes talked to Horridge in far-off tones about her family who had all disappeared in camps, some in Poland, some in Germany. She herself had come to New York in 1939. She had studied psychology, seeking elucidation that already lay in the Talmud. She had practised that art in the 'forties. She had been asked to make a case study of Senator MacCarthy. It had bored her. Now she stayed in her penthouse, smoked Camels and drank Old Kentucky Bourbon. She had a Puerto Rican maid. Occasionally the lady, not the maid, descended to Harlem and brought back a stud. She liked to wear African bangles in bed. After they had made love she paid the man and rang the bell for the Puerto Rican maid to show him out. Sometimes she imagined there was then an interlude. The stud had accompanied the girl to her room. She found this mildly exciting at first, then more so. Eventually she became aware it was more exciting than what the Negro did to her. So she stopped going to Harlem. She recognised this was selfish. Horridge also had been spending afternoons with the maid, but it seemed she didn't yet know about that. She slept in the afternoons, reading much of the night. Horridge and the lady started injecting each other with cocaine. It had curiously no effect on either of them. Perhaps they were cheated by the suppliers. Finally she told Horridge he must go. There was a scene. He owed that to his view of himself. Then he left. He asked the Puerto Rican maid to visit him in the Hotel Chelsea where he went to stay. She promised to come. She didn't keep the promise and he forgot about her. He was now involved with the daughter of a dry-goods millionaire who had ambitions as an actress. She looked more like Tippi Hendren than Tippi Hendren really did. She lacked a sense of humour and showered four times a day. One afternoon Horridge opened the *New York Daily News* and read that the Jewish lady's apartment had been burglarised. The Puerto Rican maid had been found with a knife in her belly. She wasn't expected to live. She was declared to be a heroin addict and five months pregnant. The Jewish lady's body had been thrown from the window overlooking the East River. It had caught on a fire escape twelve floors down. She had hung there—the pathologist expertly opined—for several hours before death. It was probable that she had cried out but there was no one to hear. All the other floors in the block were given over to offices.

Horridge read this while the Tippi Hendren-blonde whose name was Lois was showering for the third time that day. He tore the plastic curtain aside and had her up against the wall under the running water. It was almost rape.

The next day he left New York.

'Are you absolutely sure it's safe?' Jeremy blushed as he put the question, 'I mean are you absolutely certain he's reliable?'

'Baby boy, jus' yo' trust li'l ol' Wilson.'

'I wish I didn't want it but I do. Is he at all like Benny?'

'Like as two peas.'

'And you're quite sure it's . . . he hasn't got a father or anything has he?'

'Don' yo' worry yor pretty head. 'Slong's the money's okey-dokey this cutie's right. I bring him this very afternoon.'

'Oh, Wilson . . . you will see he's got a surplice?'

'Trust me, baby blue.'

Lady Gertrude was remembering too.

She had gone to the Ball reluctant, as she now moved through life. She was in rebellion against that sort of thing. Instead she had a studio in Flood Street, paid for unwillingly by Daddy, a country squire by conviction, whose money came however from the manufacture of boot polish. They were a nest of artists in that house and the street was a rookery. They all despised notions of good form and were contemptuous of those whose slavery to convention caused them to dress for dinner. They felt they were poor and had made sacrifices.

'I refused,' Gertrude frequently proclaimed, 'a season. It's positively obscene, the very idea.'

'Out of the Ark,' her friend Nancy would assure her.

It didn't occur to Gertrude till sometime during the Spanish War that Nancy was what was then called Sapphic, but she admired the panache with which she wore trousers even when going to visit her folks in the country. She herself had never quite dared to wear them west of Paddington.

She sat at her dressing-table looking beyond at the blank face of Norfolk. She held a pressed flower in her hand. The scent from a potpourri filled the air.

She had refused Miles at that dance and to annoy him started to flirt with Edgar Beazley. Miles had sulked. To sweeten him she had in a sudden access of high spirits poured sugar on his head. Never able to look a spaniel in the eye since. Miles had gone to the Federated Malay States. He had died in a Japanese camp. They had told her his weight at death was just under seven stones.

Miles had had no sympathy with people who didn't wear white ties at dances. Someone had presented himself in a dinner-jacket and Miles had called him impudent. She had laughed; in easy mockery.

She could date the decline in her reputation as a serious artist from three portrait heads of Miles she had done from memory in 1949.

She put her head on the dressing-table so that her cheek rested on the potpourri.

Atwater, reluctant, had done a round of agencies. Some had unnervingly promised that they might have something in a few weeks when things looked up. 'There's lots of Arab money on its way,' they said. 'May lead to something, can't tell.' More often, however, they shook their heads and sneered. One or two remarked, 'If you'd money to invest we could take it off you.'

It appeared that provision for the future was no nearer. The child however was. Nothing could postpone the march towards its birth. Polly was now reporting to the clinic at fortnightly intervals. She was becoming edgy. This upset Atwater. Moreover, she had received a letter from Mrs Hedge. It was not friendly. It spoke of Mrs Hedge's extreme disappointment and disillusion. This, as Atwater pointed out, was strange. Mrs Hedge was fond of telling the public, perfect strangers when you came to look at it, that they could not continue to live in a fools' paradise of their own making but must face up to grim reality.

'She shows,' Atwater said disapprovingly, 'a marked disinclination to take her own medicine. On reflection I'm not at all surprised.'

Mrs Hedge was compelled to sever relations with Polly. She stood aghast at Polly's selfish irresponsibility.

She herself had been seen at a number of Blueprint for Britain meetings with the apple-cheeked daughter of a Rural Dean.

Atwater was now coming from a meeting with a self-styled Communications Tycoon. He had proposed himself as a Political Adviser. They had met one day in the bar of the Hyde Park Hotel and discovered an old acquaintance.

'It should not be forgot,' Atwater said, frowning over his spectacles, 'that we were once slung into each other's arms outside the Sun in Splendour in Notting Hill. We have moved in different directions, life's currents have carried us asunder, since those halcyon days of boyhood, but our paths have now crossed again.'

The tycoon was slow to recall the incident.

'Sun in Splendour?'

'I saved you from landing on your arse in the gutter,' Atwater reproved him. 'Or perhaps your nose. With the water that has passed under the bridges I don't now recall which way round you were flying through the air.'

'Sun in Splendour?'

The tycoon wrinkled his brow, doubtless striving to summon up the memory of those pubs whence he had been slung a couple of decades back.

'We are older now,' Atwater said. 'We can no longer lead the carefree life of youth. Weighty responsibilities oppress us. In short, I need a job.'

'Sun in Splendour you say?'

'In Notting Hill.'

'Used to own property there. Got out of House Property though. Gets you a bad name, House Property.'

'You flew through the air with all the nonchalant and graceful abandon of youth.'

'Suppose,' the tycoon, a man of decision, consulted a pocket book, 'you meet me Friday 12.45 for a general discussion.'

Atwater was puzzled. Almost baffled. He had approached the tycoon (recently elevated to the House of Lords) purely from boredom, hoping for little more than a couple of drinks.

'What should I ask for?' he said to Polly.

'I think you should become a political correspondent,' she said. 'I've been thinking and that's a job that requires absolutely nothing—not even news-sense—beyond the ability to fill a column with whatever you fancy once a week. Down your street, ducky.'

Atwater hesitated. 'Is it,' he said, 'not perhaps a little sordid? Think of the scoundrels I would have to mix with. Is that what you would choose for your child's father?'

'Yes.'

'As you like.'

'So I wondered if you would be a lamb and take me out to lunch first?'

'Lunch?'

Colonel Beazley's hand flew to his moustacheless upper lip.

Clare's arrival had caused a sensation in the lobby below.

'I foresee a happy ending,' motherly Mrs Hatchett, the close-fisted proprietrix of the Bellevue remarked, sighing.

'We've been worried about you, Colonel, me and Polly that is. Polly hasn't been able to sleep at nights, as for me . . .'

Clare sank on to a yellow sofa and stretched her arms along the back.

'I've missed you more than I can say.'

The Colonel gulped.

'It's terribly bad for you,' Clare continued, 'shutting yourself away like this. I've been dreaming about you. It got to such a stage that I said to myself, this is too silly, ducky, you've got to do something, so I jumped into a taxi and whooshed to Victoria and here I am. I thought perhaps the Metropole.'

'God.'

'I thought perhaps smoked salmon, a little plump lobster and then *filet de bœuf en croûte*, something deliciously simple. So be an angel and put on your moustache. A lamb-like hock with the fish and a bloody old Burgundy with the beef. And I think you should ask them to get your bill ready. I've decided it's not good for you, this place.'

'Who the hell . . .?'

'I dote on you ducky when you bluster but they tend to close the kitchens at the Metropole ridiculously early, it causes an awful fuss with week-enders who never think of time, love, you know.'

Outside on the promenade the Boy held a knife against the girl's throat. She stood pale, thin and unmoving. The grey wind swept last Sunday's *People* round their ankles. Absorbed in their endless and immutable drama they didn't see the Colonel and Clare come out of the hotel and disappear in the taxi. They didn't see the Colonel's luggage taken away later in the afternoon's gloom. The street-lights came on, night closed in and the gulls cried.

Atwater had become a ghost.

'I've no room for a political adviser at this moment in time,' the tycoon had said. 'I'm going to be in the next government you see. That'll be any day now. We're going to set up an interim Government of National Regeneration. We'll keep the PM of course, he'll be the anchor man, but me and Mrs Hedge, we're to be the muscle.'

'Mrs Hedge and I do not see eye to eye.'

'So what? Atwater, you impress me, but don't make the mistake of thinking you're important enough to make me think you're important. Nobody's that important. Get it? Good. Now what I want's an autobiography and fast. You've got a week to do it, I'll pay a couple of thou', here's half, there's the tape recorder, now get me born somewhere solid. And listen, muscles don't necessarily agree.'

Dr Ngunga laid down his pen. All was in readiness. The skein was unravelled. Soon, he, Ngunga, would be in a position beside which even a Fellowship of All Souls paled into insignificance. A career, unparalleled in pertinacious duplicity, was to be crowned. 'Lord, now lettest thou thy servant enter into thy glory,' he hummed.

'Darling, you can't guess what I've done.'

'No?'

'Not possibly. I've been and gone and got him. Your father.'

'Daddy? Got him where?'

'Here.'

'How is he?'

Clare glanced at the figure in the brown dressing-gown.

'Overwhelmed, poorest lamb, it's been so bad for him, brooding.'

'Tell.'

'Well, you know about my dreams and gondolas, I mean. They kept on happening so eventers I decided they must mean something, I mean they must be meant. Anyway they weren't doing either of us any good, I mean there the poor lamb was in my dreams the whole time but quite quite ignorant of it all, not exactly sharing, you see, darling, well not at all in fact, and as for me, emptiness. So are you listening? What are you wearing?'

'Nothing.'

'Makes two of us, very *intime* wouldn't you say, so I just whooshed down to Brighton and prised him out.'

'Very clever, I am grateful, you can't think how.'

'So now we've set up a menage.'

'Oh good . . . what about Jeremy?'

'Poorest Jeremy, choir-boys, he was beaten up by a gang of them, in surplices, yesterday. Nothing's really safe not since we moved out of the pubs, isn't it odd . . .'

'Yes, but . . . maybe, Clare, it was our imagination then . . . what about his uncle?'

'Giles, oh Giles was just a practice oldie, do you know, Polly, I'm happy.'

'Me, too . . . in a way at least, strange, isn't it.'

Atwater said, 'The fact is, Adolf, reality's rather rum. I can detect at least three different levels.'

They were alone in the Club, four o'clock in the afternoon, the horses running only at Wincanton.

'They never should have closed Ally Pally,' Adolf said, polishing a glass with a dirty towel. 'London's not been the same since. That was the real thing. Hurst Park too, that's missed.'

'Ah yes.'

'Feel sometimes these days you're living in a dream.'

'Are things so vivid?'

Atwater knew why he came to Adolf's. Talking to Adolf was like stopping the dancing of the particles of dust lit up by the sun that came through the grimy window. It was making your life a painting in a gallery; landscape with figures; natural but out of nature.

Adolf said, 'I don't know as I'd call it vivid. Nights in the desert, lice and sand and twisted legs, they were vivid. Or the tubes in the black-out, you're too young to remember them, but they was an eye-opener, the tongues you explored. You won't believe it, I had a girl make love to me in the black-out once.'

Atwater said, 'I'm writing a book, it's the autobiography of a tycoon, it's all from my head, to make him respectable, it'll become real. I told him his childhood yesterday. Found him nodding agreement. I felt like a magician, I'd given him a childhood he'd never had, just like that. It's in his head now, he's no memory to speak of, so very malleable.'

Adolf said, 'I'd a lot of childhoods but they happened to a different person. They say you change all your cells every seven years, such a lot of nonsense. Is it true about the Colonel?'

'If people say it there's a truth. He mightn't know it though, so what are they saying?'

'That he's gone off to Venice with a tart.'

Atwater drank some gin. He nodded. It didn't seem worth explaining who Clare was; she would stay a tart for Adolf. It made him feel virtuous to think of women as tarts, and, as for himself, it had by the reckoning he'd quoted been a completely different set of cells, quite another Adolf, that had been fined seventeen times for importuning in Leicester Square.

'Well,' said Adolf, 'he wasn't doing himself any good in that hotel in Brighton. "Colonel," I said to him, "it's not the way you think it is or I wouldn't be here." He recognised that but he didn't feel it.'

'Yes, you've got to experience. My tycoon's having a great time, happy as a sandboy, experiencing the childhood I've given him. And talking of giving some more gin would be welcome.'

'Where it's going to end I just don't know. The way things are going I don't feel safe any more. Anyway. There's Stevie taken up with a nigger and Jeremy, a real gentleman that, from Shropshire I'm told, beaten up by choir-boys—it's a different class you get in the choir these days—and I was hearing on the wireless that there's a new Puritanism on the way. Say what you like, Mr Atwater, it's not nice. And I'm told you're getting married.'

'On Thursday.'

'Be the end of you in the Club I dare say. They say the new police'll close it anyway. I don't have what I used to have to offer, that's a fact.'

VI

To Atwater's surprise the marriage was in fact fixed. Polly had been sufficiently reassured by the tycoon's down payment of a thousand pounds in used notes to decide to commit herself. Besides, a friend dating from her political secretary days had advised it. Things might become tough for unmarried mothers, he had suggested.

'There's a new corps of women police,' he had said, 'I don't like the sound of them. Your Mrs Hedge is involved. She says we must stamp out laxity if the moral fibre of the nation is to be restored. I thought you would know about it.'

'Things move fast, Mrs Hedge and me, we're not on speakers now.'

'*Tiens*, it's probably revenge then, a kind of Wilde justice. The old girl's put together, welded you might say, an unholy alliance of virgins, Lesbians and vicar's wives, not necessarily exclusive categories, of course. You heard what they did to Richie's wife when they caught her whoring?'

'No.'

He whispered in her ear.

'Heavens. I expect they got a kick out of that.'

'No doubt.'

'Still that sort of stuff doesn't exactly spread sweetness and light. I think, Atwater darling, we'd better get married in church.'

'If we are going through with it, I should certainly prefer the ceremony took place in church. Registry offices remind me of Tote betting. Have you a parson in mind?'

'Perhaps we should go down to Norfolk?'

Atwater nodded and went for a walk by the river in the rain.

Leaves were beginning to appear on the trees and the air was soft and English. He passed a park where two or three schoolboys were throwing a cricket ball about. A blond boy emerged wearing pads and carrying a bat. He wiped the misty rain from his brow.

'It's stopped,' he called, 'we could start again.'

A slim dark-haired, olive-skinned boy took a few steps and, with a wheeling action, left-armed, bowled at him, a looping flight. The blond boy, on the front foot, leant into the stroke, driving gently and correctly towards mid-off. The bowler skipped to his left and, pouncing on the ball, made to throw down an imaginary wicket. A stout man with a pipe in his mouth came to the door of the hut that served as a pavilion. He looked up at the clouds, strato-cumulus, still heavy with rain.

'There's no hope, I'm afraid, chaps, we'll have to call it a day, Jenkins go and get the stumps in.'

'Oh sir,' said the blond boy, 'please.'

There were piles of sawdust behind the wickets at either end of the pitch. A thrush was singing lost in the lime tree.

Atwater walked on to the evening sound of bells. Pigeons were black as rooks against the dulling sky.

'Atwater,' wrote the Jewish young man, running his tongue across his lips, 'ran his tongue across his lips. Below him the river swirled grey and malevolent with an oily translucence that reminded him of all the whores he had enjoyed only in his concupiscent imagination. Desperately he began to masturbate standing there on the parapet of the bridge. The trembling voices of deliria chanted encouragement and derision.

'"Go to it, Atwater. King of the pansies, king of the poofs, the great whore-monger, the drug addict, the drunk. He won't have the nerve, lay you odds."

'Another voice chipped in, in plain.

'"Piccadilly Circus, Piccadilly Circus, Atwater's old friend, Sebastian Carson, never liked to cross Piccadilly Circus in his last years because he didn't like to confront Atwater, the newspaper-seller with no nose, yes that's what Atwater, king of the pansies, king of the New York vice ring, was reduced to, selling newspapers in Piccadilly Circus with no nose, and his old friend Sebastian Carson . . ."

'"Sir Sebastian Carson."

'"Correction taken, never liked to cross the circus, instead he went underground. Imagine his horror though when one day what should he find there but Atwater with no nose, syphilis you know, injecting himself with heroin."

'"Atwater was once in bed simultaneously with Clare and Jeremy."

'"Jeremy from Shropshire?"

'"Jeremy from Shropshire. Which did he fancy? Did he roger Clare or bugger Jeremy? He was too drunk to manage either. That, chaps, was Atwater, the Queen's own stallion of the Queen's Elm bar."'

The Jewish young man took the paper from the typewriter. He lit a Woodbine and read what he had written. He saw that it was good. There is a truth here, he muttered, that passeth all understanding.

His bed-sitting-room in Shepherd's Bush was grey and smoky with a smell of underpants and cigarette stubs. One wall was covered with *Playboy* cut-outs. Another was lemon yellow as sorrow. Outside the window, in the May evening, the starlings gathered. There was a withered plane tree in the mean square. He put his hand through his hair, scattering the dandruff. In the room above an old man walked restlessly to and fro. Occasionally he cried out to his wife. She had been dead many years but the old man still called to her as the street-lights lit up the empty night. In his room, as in the room below and up and down the stairs, milk bottles and Guinness bottles and bottles with peeling labels, but which had contained pale ale, stood arrayed. The young man never went to the pubs now being absorbed in writing but his old neighbour would bring him beer.

'How's it going?'

'It's pursuing its inexorable way.'

'It's a great talent you have there laying the Lord's patterns on the paving-stone. You'll remember what Shelley said, "Poets are the unacknowledged legislators of mankind."'

The young man would smile and uncap a bottle.

"'Tis a great consolation to make sense of the world and a great gift the Lord has bestowed upon you and something of meaning and order it is you've returned to my bleak and melancholy existence.'

The news of the wedding plans had revived Lady Gertrude. A Great Dane bitch was whelping too and though inclined to confuse the events her new animation was perhaps a tonic. That was the vicar's opinion; for what such opinions are worth.

To mark her renaissance she had abandoned tea and returned to brandy.

She despatched a telegram to the Colonel who was now staying at the Gritti in Venice.

'Imperative you return immediately stop give bride away stop the bitch to be bridesmaid stop.'

It was understood that by bitch she meant Clare. This was an error though excusable. Lady Gertrude, who in her recent wanderings had gone far beyond human bonds, saw no absurdity in having a pregnant Great Dane as bridesmaid. Indeed it struck her as apposite that the two, one great with child, the other great with pup, should be so associated. Had anyone realised this was how her mind was working it might have been suspected that her recovery was not all it seemed.

She operated however with brisk efficiency. She tested the vicar on his knowledge of the marriage service and ability to conduct it. When he confessed himself rusty (for his few parishioners under eighty-five copulated without benefit of clergy; such was the decay of rural England) she gave him a swift rehearsal. She ordered and then issued invitations. She employed a firm of private detectives to seek out Horridge whom she had designated usher, chucker-out and master of ceremonies. She engaged a second firm to screen the guest list and excise pansies from it; and a third to screen the other two. Finding that no bakers now existed in Norfolk or indeed East Anglia capable of baking a wedding-cake she imported a marvellous confection from Vienna. She consulted wise women and demanded horoscopes and ordered Polly to procure a sample of Atwater's hair.

'It must be taken from his head while he sleeps,' she said. 'Hair that has fallen out is worse than useless, being deceptive.'

She undertook to organise Polly's trousseau and commissioned a Paris house to make a marvellous dress in biscuit organdie. (At the same time she ordered a brindle robe of strange design which confirmed the maestro of the house in the worst suspicions he had ever entertained concerning *les demoiselles anglaises*; he took to his bed and died within the moon.)

She insisted that Polly invite Mrs Hedge.

'She shall be shown,' she said, 'that the County remains the County. Blood will tell the impudent counter-jumper.'

Such was the vehemence of her delivery that neither Polly, Atwater nor the vicar was certain whether a comma succeeded the word tell, or not.

All in all, she became a bit excited.

'Valium's what she needs,' Polly said.

'I shall pray for her.'

Atwater pondered on hammer-blows.

He had completed his literary assignment. Lord Bruggles ('I wanted a name that would sound the common touch—I used to be Symington-Lejeune in the old days, but my advisers thought it sounded too Jamaican') expressed himself well-pleased. He invited Atwater to dine at the Ritz.

'Bring your girl,' he said. 'We'll make a night of it.'

'Well,' Atwater said, 'it's probably not what it sounds like.'

'Since I'm in pig, filthy luck on him if he does.'

They arrived in the Pink Bar to discover to their surprise that another guest was Dr Ngunga. There were also two tarts, exiguously clad, their charms, which were abundant, most generously displayed. Atwater's autobiography had spoken in fervent terms of Lord Bruggles's Chapel background— 'that simple red-brick mission-house where on an English Sabbath the voice of God silenced t'horns of t'mill', and of Lord Bruggles's sacred mother—'she taught me to respect womankind wherever and in whatever condition I should come across them; and this simple lesson, too often and too easily forgotten by the younger generation, I have always cherished in my memory. T'mills in that Yorkshire town might be dark and Satanic but they shone with the light of a true candle against the darkness of the pleasure houses of Sodom and Gomorrah.'

Dr Ngunga said, 'Where could this happen but in England? As I have long maintained, the glory of England is its concentric, intertwining social circles, not, *bien entendu*, like those so marvellously portrayed by the divine Alighieri in his matchless and indeed unrivalled *Inferno*, but rather, my friends, like those equally richly but with a quite different delicacy delineated by the sagacious Mr Powell (Tony not Enoch),' he paused to titter, 'in his ever so intricate, gossamer-like elucidation of the mores of those not quite dinosaurs, the seedier section of the aristocracy.'

'Doctor,' said the blonde tart, inclining a quite remarkable breast to him and exhaling admiration, 'my friend here isn't intellectual like me.'

'Think nothing of it,' the doctor proclaimed, flashing a billboard smile. 'I come to meet this brilliant, as yet unsung but ever so soon to be carolled, litterateur, and who do I find but my old companion in arms, the redoubtable and versatile Mr Atwater. It would be sufficient to restore my faith in human nature were it indeed possible for so sanguine a nature as mine ever to have lost it. And the delectable Miss Polly too, soon, or so I gather, to be plucked as the prudent partner of your blood, my dear Atwater, as the great Tennyson so aptly if unromantically put it, and in less time after the happy day than is conventional, such are the beneficent generosities of an all-seeing Providence, to enter, I perceive, into the saintly state of Motherhood. Let us drink champagne.'

Since the last Atwater and Polly had heard of Dr Ngunga was the news that he was flying for his life, it was surprising though agreeable to find him in the Ritz. It confirmed an old undergraduate maxim of Atwater's that the one place in the world where nothing unpleasant could ever happen, the protected realm whither one should resort on H-Day, was the American Bar of the Ritz. He had spent many hours there in his more provident youth.

Once an American, hearing him order a Gin Rickey, had said, 'What sort of a drink is that, sir?'

'Mr Atwater and his friends,' Laurie had remarked, 'were weaned on Gin Rickeys.'

Anxious to reconcile the old with the new, Atwater said, 'Postpone champagne. Let us drink Gin Rickeys.'

'Gin Rickeys?' the other tart, a West African who seemed to go by the name of Coal Black Missy, inquired. 'What sort of a drink is that?'

'Like Mother's milk,' said Atwater.

'Mother's milk,' sighed Coal Black Missy; she rolled her eyes, effortlessly taking a couple of centuries off her culture. 'Ah reckon ah prefer champagne. Bein' a single gel, y'knaw.'

'And not, I'm sure, for want of asking,' Dr Ngunga said.

'Why, Doctor, are you a-propositionin' me now?'

'Would that I were,' the doctor said, 'but *force majeure*. It is remarkable the self-restraint the ladies show now. Time was, you will remember, your lordship . . .'

'Don't you call me that, Seth lad, it still feels like a new pair of clogs . . .'

'How when we were green in youth, our salad days, as the Swan has it, marriage was every maiden's dream, but now . . . *eheu fugaces, Postume* . . .'

Atwater said, 'It's not so much a positive disinclination to the state,' he laid his hand between Polly's thighs, 'as the result of the reflection that they can now go where they like unescorted.'

Lord Bruggles said, 'Marriage is the rock of a Christian family.'

Atwater, though pleased to find him talking in the character he'd created for him, said, 'And, like other rocks, causes many a shipwreck.'

Polly said, 'There comes a day when it seems the thing to do, but I can't help thinking of poor Mr Hedge when we talk of marriage.'

The blonde tart wriggled, 'You know, dear, I come all over goose-pimples when I think of being a bride. Goose-pimpled to my tits. Orange-blossom's always meant a lot to me.'

'In my country,' said Coal Black Missy, 'flirtation's a smokescreen, a wedding's not the work of an idle moment.'

'Here neither,' Polly said, 'I hope you'll both come to ours.'

They drank three Gin Rickeys apiece, Coal Black Missy withdrawing her reservations, then a magnum of Perrier Jouet, and ate some sole cooked rather badly in a turgid sauce. However the leg of lamb was vernal and the claret deliciously autumnal so that their spirits, depressed by the sole, rose again.

Lord Bruggles made a short speech about young couples setting out on life's great adventure, but lost his way despite determined prompting from the doctor, and sat down again, calling lustily for Port and Stilton.

'This,' he said three times, fondling Coal Black Missy, 'is a typically English dinner.'

'Would you like me to dance on the table?'

'Later,' Atwater suggested, 'and perhaps another table.'

'And folks say England is finished, no sir.'

'I had dinner at Maxim's once, you should have seen me, doctor, I was dressed to kill . . .'

'Ah . . .'

'In a feather boa . . .'

'A feather boa . . .'

'Know a story 'bout a boa.'

'Really?'

'Quite suitable. Chap had a boa as a pet. He played the French horn.'

'A remarkable snake.'

'Quite.'

'Very.'

'No, only quite, because one day it got mixed up in the folds of the horn and indeed swallowed by it. So in despair he telephoned his friend or, perhaps, being French, sent a pneumatique, saying "*ah, que le son du boa est triste au fond du cor*". Ah well it makes a better story if you know your Gerard de Nerval.'

'Gerard de Nerval, ah'll say, what a boy.'

Coal Black Missy whooped and threw a glass up at the ceiling.

Clearly the evening was working up to be a traditional success.

Unfortunately, before the night was much further advanced, Lord Bruggles had been arrested by a traditionally minded policeman for absent-mindedly propositioning a nice young lad in a canary-coloured jumpsuit in Leicester Square. Lord Bruggles explained in a heavy Midland manner that he had thought the lad was his girl who had been with him at his shoulder a moment back. He had not realised, he said, that she had dropped behind. They had all drunk a bit. He could see the policeman was a sport; and to prove it he waved a fat wallet about suggestively.

His appreciation of the situation was faulty, however, and Lord Bruggles, the destined saviour of the Nation, the bastion of the Blueprint for Britain movement, spent the night in a cell and appeared at Bow Street the next morning. The magistrate there, until recently proprietor of the Happy Valley Chinese restaurant but a novice at the judging game, anxious to show neither fear nor favour, etc, committed him for trial with a few choice observations. Worse, he refused bail on the flimsy and facetious grounds that bail would give a man of Lord Bruggles's standing every opportunity to tamper with witnesses. This was a temptation he had decided to guard him against.

148

'It is,' Atwater said, 'yet another example of the mutability of fortune.'

'Mrs Hedge will be gnashing her teeth, poor thing.'

'If she knows how to. I don't. It will probably set back the coup. It makes my book look even sillier.'

'Still, the money's safe.'

'Oh yes, the money's safe.'

Horridge heard of the arrest on his transistor. He laughed so hard he all but ruptured himself. Listening to his transistor gave him an uncomfortable feeling of communion with Harriet. He was trying to kick the habit.

'They'll have to go through with it without me,' the Colonel said. 'I can't risk being in the same county as the bitch. She's been too much for me, that's all there is to it.'

'Then I'll fly back for the day, wouldn't miss it for worlds, not seeing Atwater in a morning coat, can you resist that, aged person, what fortitude.'

They were sitting outside Rosati's in the Piazza del Populo. The Colonel had gone off Venice, having got very drunk one night and stumbled into a canal.

'It's not so much the wet, it's the stench,' he said and insisted they take the morning *Rapido* to Rome.

'All right, you do that, we'll ransack Gucci and the Via dei Coronari for gifts.'

Clare looked at him doubtfully.

She distrusted his air of unstudied normality.

The old booby was up to something.

Richie kicked his heels in his prison cell. He wished he was kicking his fifth wife. Or his fourth. Come to that, any of the bitches.

Aloysius ordered a morning suit in sumptuous grey velvet. He would wear his pink ruffled shirt and the yellow top hat he had bought in an auction at Sothebys. It had once belonged to Lord Lonsdale.

'Wilson,' he said, 'you is sometimes well-dressed, possessin' as you do a nat'ral inherited flair, but you is totally ignorant o' de philosophy o' clothes. You don' know Carlyle.'

'Aloysius baby, ah ain't never been north o' Potter's Bar an' ain't plannin' on goin'. 'Cept for this weddin'. That's an exception, bein' de weddin' o' de century.'

'Wilson, you is plumb ignorant. Carlyle was a writer.'

'Ah thought it was a football team, it's on de coupon.'

'My, my, Wilson, you answer me jist one question . . . What is a dandy? Ah thought as much, you ignorant nigger . . . a dandy, Wilson, is a clothes-wearin' man.'

'Fancy that, Stevie baby, youz a dandy.'

Invitations to the wedding proliferated. Atwater, paying a sentimental visit to the Turkish Baths, invited not only Mac and Bartholomew the Door and Terry his masseur but also the one-eyed Marquess of Turriff whom he had found chatting up Terry. The Marquess seemed pathetically grateful for the invitation. He said he had found a coolin' towards the aristocracy in gamblin' circles. Atwater reassured him. Peers of the realm were welcome in the betting-shops and pubs he himself used. It occurred to him that it might be a kindly action to give the Marquess an introduction to Adolf's club. There he might find his heart's desire. The Marquess was dubious; rightly so. Atwater had misinterpreted his approach to Terry. It had been mere routine. So deeply was the Marquess depressed by his ugliness and lack of sexual attraction that soliciting had become a reflex action. He bought more newspapers at odd hours of the night than any other peer in London.

Atwater, worried, took him instead to Finch's.

Jeremy was at the bar, pinkly podgy. It was like seeing the Union Jack or hearing Big Ben. He said, 'Going to be quite a thrash, your wedding. Is Clarici really coming? I miss the girl.'

Atwater said, 'Jeremy, there are just two things I want to say. First, you cannot run with the hounds and hunt with the hare. The second is this: where are the remnants of my grand-dam's estate?'

'Hardly the time or place to discuss that, old boy.'

'But you are never to be found in your office now.'

'Well, not in the circs, hardly surprising, I'd say.'

'This fellow Bruggles,' the Marquess said. 'You believe what they say about him?'

'Up to a point. D'you know him?'

'Hardly say that, I've met him at the odd nocturnal news-stand but can't say I know him. Fact is, you can't tell these days whether you know anyone or not. In the old days it was easy. Fellow had been at school with you, or rowed in the same eight, or had the next butt, or served in the regiment. Or you'd heard someone say he was a Harrow man. You could always place him. Not now.'

'Ah time,' Atwater shook his head.

'Pub isn't the same without Richie,' said someone none of them had ever seen.

Jeremy put forward Shropshire as an area that had escaped the decadence the Marquess was describing. The Marquess had cousins there. They began happily to explore connections. Atwater looked deep into his Guinness. There were faces in the foam.

The pub was becoming noisier with the peculiar empty mirth of Saturday noon-time. The bed-sitters had spewed out the bachelors in search of the supermarket and greengrocer. The shopping done, they now assembled here. Regulars stretched along the bar, greeting each other's girl-friends, ex-girl-friends, uneasily divorced wives, with loud cries that proclaimed but did not express undying affection.

'Barbara, my only girl . . .'

'Christ, Ronnie, was pissed last night . . .'

'So she said to me . . . zip me down . . .'

'Jane come and give me a comforting wet kiss . . .'

'Well I wasn't taking that from an A1 bitch even if she is a producer's daughter . . .'

'Christ, you've been invisible since Kookaburra, what brings you to this waterhole . . . darling, this is Jake, you know, that Jake . . .'

'Oh Jake . . .'

'Old Bill . . .'

'I threw her clothes out of the window, that's what I fucking did . . . her nightie caught on a passing bus, I split myself, I tell you I fucking split myself . . .'

'Christ, I left the Beeb years back, I'm a freelance now, give me liberty I said or give me . . . mine's a pint of red . . .'

'That's seven pints of red, four whiskies, a gin and it, three gin and tonic and a coke, sure that's all you want, Penny, can't persuade you . . . oh, and a cheese sandwich . . .'

'That'll be five-forty-seven, sir.'

'Shit, I'm fucking emigrating.'

'Jesus . . . cheers . . .'

'Mud in your eye you old bastard . . .'

'So she said to him why don't you go screw a cook?'

'Screw a cook?'

'That's what the girl said . . .'

Atwater hearkened. The beer and whiskies till closing-time, the Chinese restaurant or Pizza Parlour perhaps, or simply, after the cheese sandwiches, the toddle homeward with the quart of Watney's or bottle of Spanish red. The sleep on the grey-pillowed divan with the telly silent and the curtains only half-drawn.

Decidedly it was time to get married. But it was hard to leave.

'*Ah, que le son du corne est triste au fond du bois.*'

Mrs Hedge felt bitter.

She tabulated her grievances:

1 Polly's unprincipled defection.
2 Lord Bruggles' arrest. As a consequence she had received a telephone call from the Prime Minister saying he thought the coup should be postponed. She had been unable to

make the old booby see that the coup was aimed at his government. What made it worse was that she could hear the water lapping in the bath as he spoke.

3 Special Branch was proving unaccountably dilatory in prosecuting its researches into Atwater's murky past. MacGilchrist was not only a broken reed, but dragging his heels to boot.

4 Mr Hedge had not only failed to return, but had been seen flaunting himself with an only too clearly consenting coloured youth.

5 Conversely, the apple-cheeked daughter of Rural Dean Cox, a real pippin, was playing hard to get.

6 A certain Dr Ngunga had called on her to discuss the possibility of arranging her kidnapping. It was all the rage, *tout à la mode*, was how he'd put it with a dark nod. Mrs Hedge had responded with all the enthusiasm of her fervent and poetic nature. She was even prepared to accept a temporary separation from the apple-cheeked Miss Cox. Then the dusky doctor (for so she had come to think of him) had telephoned to say it was all off. Their accountants had turned the scheme down. The rewards, they felt, would be inadequate and, since the last Budget, kidnapping expenses were no longer deductible.

Little wonder that Mrs Hedge felt frustrated. She gnashed her teeth, wept and occasionally wailed a bit.

The only item on the bright side was the disappearance of that dangerous lunatic, her constituency chairman.

Meanwhile, deep in flattest Norfolk, Lady Gertrude's excitement was reaching a peak that seemed to the vicar at least hysteria. Her activity was incessant. She had hired a troupe of maids to sweep the house. Then in a self-defeating reversal of policy she had liberated all the Danes from store. She had hired a butler, a wondrous fellow of inscrutable mien, in fact, though his dignified silence had hidden the secret from a dozen noble employers, a monoglot Albanian.

Despairing of detectives she had enlisted all the county's boy scouts and despatched them in search of Horridge after exhortation which led a literary and bespectacled couple to confuse that great anarch with the Holy Grail; a confusion which was to bring the gallant pair to a watery grave (in a level lake) thus casting, as Clare wittily put it, a damper on proceedings.

Despite all, Lady Gertrude was not happy. She felt something, besides Horridge, was missing. On the Thursday before the ceremony, as the guests began to gather, as dancing commenced on the village green, as the pubs began to lash out their wedding ale, a special Norfolk brew, dating (so 'twas said) from the wedding of George, Prince of Wales with Mrs Fitzherbert, she began to suspect that this missing ingredient in the olla podrida was a genuine enthusiasm on her part.

'I can't forget that I dislike the man intensely,' she sighed to a guest she didn't recognise, but who was in fact Harriet Horridge, revived and brought to the wedding by none other than Dr Ngunga himself.

'Atwater,' said Harriet, a loyal girl, vice-captain of lacrosse in her Cheltenham Ladies days, 'will always play the game.'

'That must be it. I felt sure there must be some identifiable reason.'

'Why, Harriet baby,' cried Aloysius, 'it's real good to see a sporting lady.'

'Flatterer.'

'You know this baby, lady,' Aloysius said, eager as ever to spread sweetness and light, 'this Missy Horridge, this real sporting lady, sure as crocodiles lay eggs she is. Ain't seen you baby in a month of witches' sabbats.'

'Oh.'

'Sure thing. Old Aloysius, he know 'bout witches' sabbats. Gwine to have his own TV spot—Voodoo hoodoo like he do—I begs yo' pardon, ladies, that's the rum speakin'—ti'le of the programme really is: who do Voodoo like he do; is a great li'l programme.'

'Rum?'

'Sure thing, lady, bes' Jamaican, Massa Atwater, he'm partial to a spot of matutinal rum.'

'Who,' said Lady Gertrude, frowning, 'exactly are you?'

'I'se Massa Atwater's maitred hotel.'

A boy scout found Horridge. He was a nasty little boy, voted by his classmates most likely to succeed.

'You've got to come down from this mountain,' he said.

'Fuck off.'

'You're required as best man now.'

'You heard.'

'Otherwise Mr Atwater will choose a black and the wedding'll be off. If it's off I lose one pound seventy-five because I'm down to sing "Oh for the Wings of a Dove".'

'Good.'

The boy scout, whose name was Harold, smirked. 'If you don't accompany me I'll tell Mrs Horridge where to find you.'

Horridge gave vent to a loud bellow. Had Harold had a classical education (in which case, of course, he wouldn't have found Horridge, so that the comparison could never have come to fruition in his mind) he would have been reminded of the roar of pain that Polyphemus the Cyclops uttered when Odysseus, or as he thought and said, Oudeis (which is Nobody) extinguished his eye with a flaming torch. And the comparison would not have been inept, for Horridge was, by this piece of childish blackmail, cast back into the darkness of incessant action. The light that he had glimpsed in his solitude was put out. His reported death, two years later, in a particularly foolish attempt to hijack an airliner on which it was supposed the director of the CIA was travelling, was the consequence of the blundering success of the boy scout, Harold.

Meanwhile, ignorant of his destiny, Horridge descended the mountain to hand Atwater the wedding ring.

'Wilt thou, Polly, take this man to be thy lawful wedded husband?'

'Absolutely.'

'I will is sufficient.'

'Shouldn't it be shall?'

'Actually, you know I've never understood shall and will, have you?'

'Well, I thought I did till I read Fowler, he has a dozen pages on them and I've been baffled ever since.'

'Nevertheless I now pronounce you man and wife.'

'Jolly good.'

'Tell me,' Atwater asked the vicar, 'are you Scotch?'

'Actually yes, but after Sherborne, the House and fifty years in Norfolk I'm surprised it shows.'

'It was that nevertheless.'

'Oh yes, indeed, very Scots that. Scots, not Scotch, you know.'

'Scotch was good enough for Sir Walter.'

'But not for us. Nevertheless let me tell you a story, dear boy, we've got a moment while your wife, indeed yes, disrobes or whatever they do. When I was a very young man I had a charge in Scotland, St Palladius was the name of the church, and I was officiating at a Church social—dreadful things so glad I've got rid of them here—anyway I announced the next item on the programme—Miss Jeannie Macpherson, I said, will now sing "The Flowers o' the Forest"—well-known lament about the Battle of Flodden, you know—a melancholy occasion, Flodden, I always think—immediately there came a stentorian voice raised—quite like one of the minor but noisier prophets—from the back of the hall—Jeannie Macpherson's a whure, it cried—well—nevertheless, I said, Miss Jeannie Macpherson will now sing "The Flowers of the Forest".'

'Admirable.'

'You see, dear boy, there is salvation in nevertheless. Remember that. Dear me, it must be quite fifty-four years since the events I relate and quite forty-three since I told the story.'

'It has,' Atwater said, 'a beautiful ring to it. May I ask a favour of you, sir, or, as you say in Norfolk I believe, crave a boon?'

'Do we? Indeed yes, dear boy, ask of me half of . . . well?'

'There is somewhere in the audience—congregation I expect you call it—a Jewish young man with a cast in his eye. Would you be so kind as to tell him that story? It will do him ever so much good. It might even save his soul.'

'Save his soul? Goodness. Naturally. It's what I'm here for. Dear me, this will be quite a treat. I haven't saved a soul in years.'

'Happy?'
'Do you know, yes.'
'Kiss me.'
'Man and wife.'
'Cor blimey.'
'Soon to be . . .'
'You say it.'
'Father and mother.'

Coal Black Missy said, 'I is happy for you and I blesses you.'

Clare said, 'Well.'

Horridge said, 'Aaaaah it's so bourgeois, but . . . babies . . . just let me steer clear of your mother baby.'

Adolf said, 'Wish I could ask you to the Club . . . but rules . . . your father's my . . . dear boy, hope you can bear up . . .'

Jeremy said, 'Terrific . . . abso-bally-lutely terrific.'

Wilson said, 'Don' worry, I'se a-lookin' after Jer an' Mervyn, Mervyn sure is orientated now, he's a changed man, darlings . . .'

Aloysius saw the sun come smilin' through and Dr Ngunga mounting a podium, said:

'Absent friends, how we must think of them now. First, Richie, that too married man, whose antipodean lusts may warn and challenge us all. Next the Colonel, pining by Tiber for his lovelier, less gaudy buttercup. Then Lord Bruggles, that staunch upholder of the common man, whose fall deplorable leaves all bereaved . . .

Then may I sing with saddest warbler's note
Of one in whom love with ambition fought,
That paragon of talents, Mrs Hedge,
Now fall'n by Fate's malice from her ledge.
Deprived of Polly whom she loved next votes,
She now upon a red-cheeked maiden dotes.
Thus proving if we still require such proof,
Great wits from Love are apt to stand aloof.
For Cupid, that wing'd boy and jealous god,
Does not mix well with politics, the sod.
And Venus, wife engendered of the sea,
Declines to shed her smile on that country
Where burning Sappho loved and (some say) sang
But all too often proved an also ran.'

He ceased. Zephyrs blew across the sward. The marquees, lamb-white as cricketers, resumed their trade. Champagne was poured. The voices silenced by oratory one by one took up the theme. For once the music was neither slow nor sad, whatever the undertones . . . nor was admiration long restrained . . .

''E do talk lovely . . .'

'Like a dream (black though he be) . . .'

'They're a fine pair.'

'Who is Ngunga . . . KGB they say. Can't help feeling though there's more to him than . . .'

'Meets the eye you mean. Could be.'

'Like I've always said, all sex is politics . . .'

Atwater, hearing, nodded. Marcus Aurelius had said the same thing, in different words as befitted different ages . . .